and Lies
(The Secret They Kept
Book 2)

All copyright © 2022 Joanne Saccasan All rights reserved. No part of this book may be used or reproduced in any way without permission except in the case of quotations or book reviews. This book is a work of fiction. Name, characters, businesses, organisations, places, events, locales and incidents are either the product of the author's imagination or used in a fictitious manner. Any resemblance to an actual person, living or dead, or actual events or locales is entirely coincidental.

For information contact:

Black Cat Ink Press

https://blackcatinkpress.com/

J.S Ellis

https://www.joannewritesbooks.com

Cover Design by Getcovers

Edited by Three Owls Editing

Proofread by Sianisel

ISBN: Ebook: 978-9918-9555-1-0

Paperback: 978-9918-9555-0-3

Chapter One

The cruise horn blared and I yawned while standing next to my parents as we prepared to disembark. I had slept badly; my sleep had been wretched ever since that day. Last night, I had yet another bad dream of being chased down the street by my seemingly sweet, kind neighbour, who turned out to be the opposite. She haunted me. *They* haunted me, that strange family. Though the one who haunted me the most was their son. It was only eleven in the morning, and I already was craving a drink. I drank more than I liked to admit these past few months. It had been exactly a year since Amelia Jones and her husband, Henry Jones, were arrested, and both were serving a lengthy sentence in prison.

We slowly made our way down the ship, my parents and I. They went on holiday every year on a cruise, and they suggested I should go with them, as it would do me good. I was self-employed as a freelance digital marketer, a job I could do anywhere globally – not that I would work while on holiday. I thought it was a good idea to sit and lounge in the pool area with a decadent and refreshing cocktail in my hand.

My house in Greenwich was up for sale, but my realtor couldn't sell it, not after it had been connected with a missing woman who later was found dead. Who would want to live in such a house? Now I lived in a small cottage in Highgate, thanks to my parents who helped me with the purchase of the house. It wasn't as great as my last house, but I didn't care, as long as I had a roof over my head. After going through traumatic events, you stop caring about things that seem so petty. I was ultimately different from the woman I was before.

I parted ways with my parents at the port, and we got in separate taxis. I glanced out the window at the passing streets. The tree leaves had shades of red and brown, with that hint of purple announcing the transition between summer to autumn. The sky was grey, and it was chilly out. The weather made me feel more miserable than I already was, and a cruise to the Greek islands had done nothing to shift my mood. The cabbie pulled over at my house, where the driver was kind enough to take the luggage out from the back even though it was small and not very heavy. I tipped him generously for his help. When I opened the door, there was a stack of letters on the floor. I told myself that I needed to get a proper letterbox as I picked up the pile of letters and wheeled my luggage to the living room.

I went to the kitchen, dumped the letters on the counter, and went to the fridge to hunt for a wine bottle. All there was in the fridge was the bottle of wine, stale bread, which I threw out, and a takeout pizza box, which I also cleared away. I opened the bottle of wine, poured it in a glass and took out my phone. I had a missed call and a text. I checked the missed call first, and I frowned. It was Mrs. Parker, my old neighbour from Greenwich.

She was in her seventies and the neighbourhood's gossip, and I was sure she was still talking about the Joneses and me to this day. I had spoken to her occasionally when she called to check up on me and fill me in on details about the neighbourhood. Each time she called, there was that heaviness, that awkwardness, like the elephant in the room. His name swirled onto my tongue each time she called to ask how I was, but I never asked about him, because I didn't want to allow her to gossip. My behaviour while living in that house had morphed from ridiculous to spying. I became the younger version of Mrs. Parker without knowing, but I didn't think she spied on her neighbours with binoculars. However, it was the fear and the desperation that made me behave that way.

I didn't want to deal with Mrs. Parker right now. The text was from Anna asking me how the holiday went, and that she couldn't wait to hear all about it. I replied that I would tell her about it over dinner. Anna replied right away asking if I was free on Friday night to come over to her place.

I attended back to my wine as I went over the mail, sighing and shaking my head. Primarily bills and junk mail. I should buy one of those stickers that said 'NO JUNK MAIL' along the letterbox. Still holding the glass of wine, I went to the bin and threw the junk mail in there as I heard footsteps climbing the stairs that led to my house. *No*, I thought, *that can't be right*. I checked the window just in case, but no one was there. I shook my head. My mind was playing tricks on me, listening to things that weren't there. Wine had become a coping mechanism for the bad dreams and paranoia. You try to move on from terrible experiences, but they never leave you.

I made a list of groceries and another list of work I had to get into, highlighting what was urgent and what could wait. Emails were always a priority, and although I had informed my clients that I would be away, it wouldn't stop them. I had temporarily disabled the email app on my phone to avoid tempting myself to read any work emails. I wanted to pretend I didn't exist, and the feeling was liberating. I attended to the shopping list first; the emails could wait a little longer. Although my appetite hadn't been all that great, I could do with stretching my legs. I grabbed my bag and caught my reflection in the mirror above the cabinet by the front door. My dark hair was shiny, my skin was tanned from all the afternoons I had lain on the deckchair, and my green eyes were clear, just a little glassy. This refreshed appearance startled me as I thought I would look much worse. The jumper was a little shabby, and the jeans were ragged and old, but apart from that, I looked healthy – a contrast to how I felt.

I opened the front door and saw that my neighbour from number seventy was out washing his car. He waved at me, and I gave him a half-hearted wave. I wasn't as chatty as I was before, and dread leapt into my stomach when I saw a neighbour out. It meant I had to be civil and talk about my day. I hoped he wouldn't come over and ask me how my holiday had gone. He went in the garage, and I sighed with relief. My eyes fell and I blinked rapidly; on the step lay a single thorny red rose, its petals in full bloom. It wasn't just any red rose. The colour was much darker – a burgundy, almost like blood. It was a gorgeous flower, and I crouched down to pick it up

'Ew,' I said, and put my pricked finger in my mouth.

I looked to my right and then to my left. Nothing out of the ordinary. *Who placed this here on my doorstep? Lucien?*

Chapter Two

Lucien… beautiful, promiscuous Lucien. He had become an obsession. Maybe he still was, but it couldn't be him. Why would he leave me a rose on my doorstep? The last time I had seen him was when I went to the house to collect my things and he was there gazing out the window – the perfect-looking son of Amelia and Henry Jones. Tall, blonde with delicate features and an innocent face that was anything but. After that day, I never heard from him again. He had nothing to tell me, not after what I put him through. His parents were in prison, and without a doubt he hated me.

It couldn't be him placing this rose here, not when he didn't know where I lived, and I didn't tell Mrs. Parker about my new location either. As paranoia swept over me, I put the rose on the cabinet and scanned the area before shutting the door, locking it and heading to the supermarket.

I picked up items and placed them back on their shelves. I was distracted, my mind elsewhere. Flashbacks played before me, seeing him for the first time in that alley and then towering over his mum, radiating shine. He was the loveliest thing I had ever seen, and he made a living out of his looks. I picked the items I needed: cheese, fruits and veg, canned tuna, and chicken pieces. As I was waiting in line, a man dressed in an excellent suit stood before me. He had light brown hair, and it looked like he was holding a six-pack of beers and a packet of Doritos. There was something familiar about that head. The man's turn came, and I yawned. I had the view of his side profile now, and it was DC Ben Miller, the detective who investigated Ed's disappearance. I glanced away, trying to conceal my face with my hair, a poor attempt when trying to avoid a detective. He had seen me, but said nothing. Maybe he didn't recognise me, but how could he forget the desperate woman he had in his police station a year ago? It was my turn, and I wheeled the trolley forward and placed my items on the conveyor belt. Ben had slid his wallet inside the inner pocket of his jacket.

'Emily Clarke?' he asked.

'Hello, Detective,' I said.

The bored checkout girl looked at me, then at him, and raised an eyebrow at the handsome man. I bet she didn't think he was a detective; maybe someone in a corporate job.

'How are you?' he asked.

'I'm fine,' I lied. 'Just got back from a holiday.' I threw my purchases in their bags, and the checkout girl didn't look as bored as her eyes slid back and forth between him and me, watching our interaction.

'Ah, that's nice. Where did you go?'

'A cruise,' I blabbered

'Hence the tan,' he said.

'Yep.'

The checkout girl told me the amount, and I handed her my credit card, which she swiped through the machine. *Should I tell him*, I thought as I entered my PIN, *about the rose I found on my doorstep?* And what? He would probably say I had a secret admirer. He offered to take the bags from me, and we exited the supermarket. I thought of what to ask him to make small talk, but I couldn't think of anything. I knew he wasn't married since I never spotted a ring.

'Are you still living at that house?' he asked.

'No, I'm living here now.'

'You live in Highgate?' he asked

'Yes.'

'I live here, too.'

What a small world.

'So, where is your car?' he asked, looking around.

'Actually, I came here by foot.'

'Let me give you a ride.'

'Oh, that's fine….' I trailed off.

'It's no trouble.'

I hadn't been out on a single date, and I had forgotten how to interact with a man. Not that this handsome detective would be interested in me. He was just being courteous. Maybe he felt sorry for me. I followed him to his silver sedan, where the car flashed and beeped when he pushed a button. He told me he had been a police officer for twelve years and was originally from

Surrey, but his parents moved to London when he was a teenager.

'I don't normally do this,' he said as I was about to step out of the car after I had thanked him.

'Would you care to have a drink sometime?'

I stared at him, not knowing what to say.

'You have my card if you decide you want to,' he blurted.

I nodded and got out of the car. I wasn't in the right state of mind to meet with men. Whatever happened to that bubbly person that I was once was? She was gone and replaced by this person I barely knew, whose life was about staying locked inside the safety of her walls.

Chapter Three

I sat on the sofa with a bottle of wine and a pot of noodles. The TV was on, but on mute as I picked up the phone and checked my Facebook page. The profile picture was still the one Lucien had taken of me. I looked confident and glamorous, unlike how I looked and felt now. I never doubted Lucien's talent, and he could pick a toad off the street and turn it into something extraordinary. He still left me as a 'friend' on Facebook. I went to his profile to see what he was up to. I didn't know why he hadn't remove me or block me. Whatever his reasoning was, this was the cord that bound me to him – the last link. His profile picture, as usual, was a stunning image of himself looking regal, gazing at the camera. He had changed it a week ago. His hair was no longer blonde, but had a touch of pastel pink. What had he done to his beautiful hair? It was still lovely, but his hair was a quality I liked about him. I went to the images, and several people had tagged him. And from what I was seeing, he seemed to be doing well, but you never know with social media. Nobody aired dirty laundry on there. He had graduated from university, but it said nothing about what he was venturing into – photography, I supposed, and modelling. There were images where he was tagged with girls and a few boys here and there. Old habits died hard.

Lucien was openly bisexual, of which Henry disapproved. Henry wasn't Lucien's biological father. He served in the army and raised another man's son, who was a model, had soft, delicate features, and slept around with both men and women. For Henry, that was unacceptable. At least Lucien killed no one – unlike his father, who pushed his son, Sylvian, down the well, even if it was by accident. He wanted to do the right thing by calling the police, but his unhinged wife had a better idea: report their son as missing while Sylvian had been down that well for ten years. I thought of Amelia's confession that Henry wasn't Lucien's biological father. That while he was away serving his country, Amelia had a fling with a man who had gotten her pregnant. Did Lucien know? Had he tried to locate his father?

I scrolled down to the images, and there was a photo of Lucien with Travis, the lad with pink hair whom he saw on and off. I checked the date, and the photos were posted two weeks ago. So, had they made up? Was that why he dyed his hair pink to match with Travis's? I went to Sasha's profile next. She kept me as a friend, but she might have forgotten she added me. She had lots of pictures with Lloyd, her boyfriend. She had lots of images of Lucien and his beautiful friend Jan, who was also a model. They were a bunch of beautiful people giving the illusion of how wonderful their lives were. Social media was an illusion. Yes, I made my living from digital marketing, but it was true.

I closed the Facebook app and took a large gulp of wine as my eyes went to the cabinet, to where the rose still lay from this morning. I stood from the sofa, walked towards the cabinet, and picked up the rose, being careful not to let a thorn prick me again. I lifted the rose to my nose and inhaled. Unlike other roses, which have a prominent smell, this rose had a light, almost non-existent scent. What sort of rose was this? I took in its dark red tone. It was a showy and proud flower. I went to the kitchen, dropped the rose in the bin, and shut the lid to pretend it wasn't there. My phone screeched, so I padded back to the living room and checked the screen. It was again Mrs. Parker. I groaned. I checked the clock on the wall, which read 9:30 p.m. *Maybe something happened,* I thought, but why would she call me? She had children of her own, even though the late Mr. Parker had long passed.

'Emily?' she shrieked in my ear.

Mrs. Agnes Parker always did this each time she called, as if not sure it was me whom she was calling.

'Agnes, hi, how are you?' I asked.

'Oh, Emily, I'm sorry to call you so late,' said the elderly woman. 'But I noticed an activity.'

I stared at the TV, which was on a rugby game, although I didn't even like rugby. *An activity*, she'd said. *Where? Why was she calling me?*

'What do you mean, "an activity"?' I asked.

'I was preparing for bed, and my bathroom window overlooks your house,' she explained.

I reached for the remote and turned the TV off.

'I was going to have a shower just now,' she added, 'and I saw someone at your house.'

I wanted her to stop saying 'my house.' Technically, though, it was still mine since it hadn't been sold yet.

'What do you mean, you saw someone?' I asked.

'A figure was moving inside… the house. I wanted to check if it was you. Maybe you came to collect something,' Mrs. Parker pointed out.

'Agnes, the house is empty, you know this,' I said.

'Oh, I don't know. I thought it could be you,' she repeated.

'Are you sure you saw someone in the house?' I asked.

Why would anyone want to go to that house? And whom?

Chapter Four

After I hung up, I sat on the sofa drinking more wine. Agnes insisted on calling the police, but I told her to leave it for now. Given how uncertain she sounded, she could have been wrong. Yet with all the strange things that had happened to me, it made me wonder. I never again stepped foot in that neighbourhood once I had packed everything. It could have been the realtor, but would he have a showing at the house at 9:30 at night? In the dark? Mrs. Parker didn't verify with me if the lights were on or not. I grabbed my phone and called the realtor.

'Hi, Gary. Sorry to call this late. I wouldn't call unless it's urgent,' I began after he picked up by the fourth ring.

'It's no problem. I'm still at the office,' he said.

He was at the office at this hour?

'What can I do for you?' he asked. 'You said it's urgent.'

'Um… a neighbour just called me. She said she had seen someone in the house and I was wondering if it was you? Did you have a showing?' I asked.

'No, I haven't had a showing at your house in weeks. I would call if there are any updates.'

'So, it wasn't you?' I asked to clarify.

'No,' he said.

I thanked him and hung up, then caught my reflection from the window. *Who could it be?*

#

The idyllic, red-brick house with a blue door stood there, welcoming me. It was cheaper than the other places I had seen when I bought it, and I should have known there was a catch. Ed told me about the house and got his realtor friend to show it to me, who mentioned nothing about the house's history. He'd told Ed, but Ed neglected to tell me, and I had to find out from Lucien that the house belonged to a missing woman. *Was it Lucien who broke into the house?* But why would an elegant twenty-seven-year-old who had a life do that? Revenge? He had to feel anger towards me and blame me somehow.

My eyes shifted to the house across the street, with its pristine yellow door. The house was in darkness, but there was no 'for sale' sign. Lucien had a beautiful apartment in Camden and didn't need a second house, although this one actually belonged to his parents. All the other houses' lights were out apart from number five, where I could make out the blurred TV. I took a step closer to the house as a shiver went through me, and I shoved my hand inside my pocket for the keys. The front door was intact when I inspected it. I took out my phone and peered at the windows using the torch.

I wasn't going to get in. Maybe there was someone there, but I didn't want to come face to face with them. Perhaps I should call the police. The rooms were empty, but why shouldn't they be? I moved my phone to what once used to be my living room. I made out the spot where Ed had hit me. All the memories played like old photographs. It felt like it had been years, not just twelve months.

I pointed the torch down and pressed my face to the window, and I blinked rapidly as an icy chill went through me. This was getting too strange. Now I was as spooked as I was alarmed. Someone was trying to tell me something, but I didn't know what. Through the beaming light of my phone, pointed at the window once more, I made out a single red rose, and from here, it looked identical to the one that was on my doorstep.

My heart jolted out of my chest as I stepped back from the window, and my feet slipped, landing me on my back in the bushes. I didn't feel any pain, but if I felt anything, it was fear. I picked myself up and ran out of there, far away from that house and from that neighbourhood.

Chapter Five

I couldn't sleep as I lay in the dark, tossing and turning with my mind churning. The moonlight reflected through my bedroom window as I ran through a mental list of suspects who could do this to me. It led to one. Lucien. He blamed me for what had happened since I was the one who tore his family apart, but his family was already broken long before I moved in. Henry was always shouting at his mother, displaying judgment on Lucien and Amelia, and well, she was nuts. His brother was dead. He had been down in that well for ten years, and thanks to me, he was found. Lucien had closure, but his parents were in prison. I didn't want to imagine what his life might have been like to visit them in such a hellish place. If he went to visit them, that is. There was no way of knowing. Despite the level of scrutiny he was under, according to his Facebook and Instagram profiles, he seemed to be doing well, but no one was going to post a selfie outside the prison with a caption that read:

Going to visit my parents in jail. #justmylife

No, of course not. The clock read 4:00 a.m. as I thought of the roses, the one in my bin and the other lying on the living room floor of my old house. What did it mean? I was too jittery to sleep. This was happening again, and I had to get to the bottom of this and get some peace. I reached for my phone that was charging on the bedside table, logged into Facebook, and went to his profile. There was nothing new. I went to Instagram next, but no update on there either. I dumped the phone back on the bedside table as if it were contaminated with a deadly disease, and dived under the covers as if going underwater.

#

The house seemed to loom over me like it grew larger while I was shrunken by its dominance. I mentally told myself it was just a house, nothing else. It was an object, and it wasn't going to hurt me. The memories would, though. I put the key in the lock, walked inside, and shut the door before anyone saw me. It was six thirty in the morning. Most of the neighbours were still in bed, and I didn't want to face them. I hoped Mrs. Parker wasn't awake already, looking through the windows and seeing me go inside. Then she'd come with her bossy and persistent knocks, as she used to do. She was the last person I wanted to deal with right now. I turned away from the front door and stared at the floor in disbelief. I forced my eyes shut and opened them again, hoping my eyes were playing tricks on me. The rose wasn't there. It was gone. Could I have been mistaken? Did I imagine it? No, I was sure there was a red rose on the floor. So, where did it go?

My body trembled as I took tentative steps, glancing around the empty living room and heading to the kitchen. The furniture I'd had was still here. I didn't see the point of having it removed. If it ever got sold, whoever bought this house could remove it themselves or keep it. I cared little about what they did. I opened the cupboards, but they were empty, as I was sure they would be. The Joneses' house was visible from the window, and a car was parked in the driveway – a smart Mercedes. Lucien? As far as I was aware, Lucien didn't own a car, but he had a driving licence and he could have bought one by now. Mercedes didn't seem his type; I pictured him driving something sportier.

I made out a woman moving about in the kitchen. I checked the time on my watch – 6:45 a.m. A man came out of the house dressed in a suit and kissed the woman on the cheek. Lucien had sold the house, from the picture I was getting, and this couple were now the new residents. If I asked Agnes, she would tell me. She mentioned nothing about the Joneses, and I never asked. So, the house of the two killers could be sold, but not mine? What was wrong with this picture? I moved away from the window and headed upstairs. The doors were all closed. I checked every room, but I found no rose, and nothing seemed to be amiss – no sign of a break-in. I went back downstairs and checked the window again, and the yellow door was now shut. Something was very wrong here, and this was far from over. Amelia coming after me and Henry's confession were just the beginning.

Chapter Six

I left the house, and Mr. Taylor was on his way out of his house from three doors down and looked at me, aghast. I muttered, 'Good morning.' I didn't see any reason to be impolite. In minutes, it would be all over the neighbourhood that I was back and crossing the street, heading towards number four, the Joneses' house. I rang the bell as Mr. Taylor stood there, still staring at me. The yellow door opened, and I thought Lucien would answer the door for a moment, but that would be ridiculous since he no longer lived there. Instead, a woman with blonde hair in her early fifties answered the door. She looked at me up and down. I knew how I must have looked to this dainty woman's eyes. I was still in my pyjamas under my oversized tweed coat and colourful bed socks and trainers.

'How may I help you?' the woman asked.

She had delicate features with green eyes, and something about her reminded me of Amelia, which reminded me of Lucien.

'Hi,' I said, trying to sound upbeat. 'My name is Emily Clarke. I used to live right across from this house,'

I pointed at the house, and the woman looked over my shoulder.

'I thought that house is for sale,' she said.

'Yes, I am the one selling it. Are you new here?' I asked.

The woman peered at me, probably questioning what business it was of mine.

'We moved here ten months ago,' she replied.

'I see. Did you, by any chance, witness any activity in my house last night?'

The woman blinked at me. 'What sort of activity?'

Mrs. Parker came out of her house dressed in a housecoat, and my heart sank. She was the last person I wanted to see. Maybe she wouldn't notice, but of course, she did as her head turned in the direction of the house, and I swear I saw her do a double take.

'Emily!' Agnes shouted.

I looked back at the woman, but the yellow door stared back at me. Not very talkative; just like Henry. Agnes crossed the street and was coming towards me.

'What on earth? What are you doing?' She looked at my questionable outfit. 'Did you go out dressed like that?'

She made it sound as if I was naked under my coat.

'I couldn't sleep,' I said. 'I kept thinking about what you told me, so I came to check the house.'

'I think you should notify the police,' she said.

I crossed my hands across my chest. 'What did you see?'

'A figure. I couldn't tell if it was a woman or a man. My eyesight isn't as good as it used to be.'

'But you are certain there was someone inside the house?'

'Yes.'

I wasn't going to mention anything to her about the rose being there last night and finding it gone this morning. The less information I gave her, the better.

'What about there?' I said, pointing at the Joneses' house. 'What happened there?'

Agnes lowered her head. 'I didn't mention anything because I didn't want to upset you, given how you felt about Lucien.'

'He sold the house?' I asked.

'Yes, to the Mitchells.'

'So, Lucien no longer lives here?'

It was a stupid question. If he sold it, he wouldn't live there.

'No, after what happened with his parents… it wasn't easy for him to lose everything at once, so he sold everything.'

'What do you mean, everything? Didn't he have an apartment in Camden?' I asked.

Agnes looked at my house, then back at me. 'The last thing I heard, he sold this house and moved out of the apartment in Camden.'

'I see.'

'Would you like to come in for a cup of tea?' she asked.

I shook my head. 'I should go.'

'I know it's none of my business,' Agnes said. 'But you should let him go. He's no good.'

Chapter Seven

I picked up the rose from the bin, placed it on the counter, made myself a cup of coffee and sat in the kitchen, staring at the flower. Roses represented great beauty, and the thorn was for sacrifice, pain and honour – an homage to Jesus Christ if going for the biblical term. Lucien was beautiful, and the thorn was for the pain I had put him through? Was it really him? I still had my doubts that he would do this. Why now? Why not sooner? How could he have known when I arrived home from the cruise? I posted a photo with my parents when I was on the cruise, but I didn't make a post that I was back in the country.

I got up from my chair, rinsed the mug in the sink, and tried to get some work done. I had a lot of catching up to do, and diving back into my work would distract me from what was going on. I spent the first hour replying to emails, setting up meetings with clients, and working on a copy for a restaurant, which took a good chunk of my time.

My phone went off, and it made me jump.

'Where are you?' Anna asked.

'Um… at home.'

Then I remembered. 'I've forgotten, haven't I?'

'Yep,' Anna said.

'I'm on my way.'

Forty-five minutes later, the taxi deposited me at a plush, red-brick apartment. The downside was it was located across the train tracks, where the block seemed to tremble each time a train rumbled by. As I rang the buzzer, a train clattered by and my hair blew with the speed – not in a way that made my hair flow like they do in commercials, but on my face. I was buzzed in and took the lift to the sixth floor. The door was ajar, and Anna stood in her living room holding a glass of wine. I accepted the wine gratefully, and she put her arms around me.

'Aw…' she said. 'How are you? How was the cruise? Tell me all about it.'

She escorted me to the white sofa where a pizza box and sushi were waiting. I told her about the cruise and the places I had seen. She told me about her work as we ate and poured glasses of wine. I even told her about running into Ben, which seemed to surprise her. I didn't mention the roses, though.

'He asked you out?' she asked. 'Oh, Em, go.'

'What? No!' I said.

'Why not? What's it going to hurt?'

'The last time, it did hurt,' I pointed out.

'That was different. He's a copper and hot, and it's just a drink,' Anna assured me.

She stood and opened the fridge, taking out a lemon cheesecake from which she cut two large pieces and then placed the plates on the coffee table. A flashback came back to me from when Anna came over after I moved into the house and Ed was away. We had taken our dessert to the living room, where Anna stayed by the window while Lucien was going at it outside with a blonde. Later she was revealed to be Julie Fulton, a girl questioned by the police regarding Sylvian's death. But, of course, she'd had nothing to do with it.

'Oh, you'll never guess who sent me a Facebook message the other day,' Anna said, snapping me back to reality.

I looked at her. 'Who?'

'Jan,' she said

I furrowed my eyebrow. 'What did he want?'

She tapped on her phone. 'It was strange. It's like he just then remembered I existed.' She handed me her phone to show me the chat that was sent three days ago.

Jan: Hey! It's been a while since we spoke.

Anna: What in the name of arse? Did you suddenly remember I'm alive!?

Jan: I have no excuses.

Anna: Well, at least you're honest.

Jan: Let me buy you a drink and make it up to you.

Anna: There is nothing to make up. We're fine.

Jan: If you insist.

I clicked on his profile and scrolled through his feed; the last update was a day ago when he posted a selfie with Lucien. There were hordes of people around them and the location read Netherlands. They were at a festival called *Darkly Fantasy*. So, Lucien was in the Netherlands?

'Are you going to meet him?' I asked.

'No, why would I?'

'Well, you were taken by him.'

'I haven't spoken to him in a year,' she pointed out.

'Why did you keep him as a friend on Facebook?' I asked.

'Well, he's very nice to look at.'

I went to his photos and stared at Jan with his luscious black hair, sensual green eyes, full lips and a face so sculpted it looked like marble. Definitely very nice to look at. Just as Lucien was, Jan could be even more beautiful. Some people were born blessed while others had to work harder on their looks. But these people were so beautiful, it was almost ridiculous. Lucien might have moved out of his apartment in Camden, but he wouldn't be so hard to track down, not with social media.

Chapter Eight

The street lamps cast an orange glow as tyres splashed on the road from the rain that had poured earlier. I felt slightly light-headed as I climbed the steps to my house and opened the door. I checked every room, but everything looked as I had left it. The empty coffee mug on the desk, my notes and the laptop still open with the screen saver on. I went to the kitchen and stopped dead in my tracks as I found the rose lying on the counter. Then I remembered I was the one who placed it there. What was I thinking? I threw the rose in the bin and voices boomed through the walls of the house next door. My neighbours, the Crofts, had a teenage boy and girl who I used to hear arguing with their parents most nights, and the son liked to bang on the doors so hard it sounded like a gunshot. It took me a while to get used to it. Tonight, they were fighting again. As I made my way to the bed, I heard the 'fuck yous' and 'fuck offs' and dropped onto the bed. I considered what Anna had told me about meeting Ben. I reached for my phone and composed a text as the banging from next door sounded once more. Then Mr. Croft yelled at his son, 'If you break one of those fucking doors, you'll pay for it from your fucking pocket.' Wasn't there a family who wasn't unhappy, who didn't have its own dysfunction?

#

The sun swept from the window, assaulting my eyes, and I rolled away from it, not noticing I was on the edge and fell off the bed. I groaned as I grabbed the sheet to pick myself up. There was a circle of my saliva on the pillow. I located the bathroom, brushed my teeth and had a cold shower. Afterward, in the kitchen, I made a cup of coffee so strong it would wake the dead. I checked my phone, and there was a text from Ben.

I'm off duty tomorrow night. How about a drink at a pub?

Ben replied to that text at 10:30 p.m. I had nothing much to do, so I *could* meet him for a drink. I checked Lucien's Facebook, and now he was actually tagged in Jan's photo. Sasha didn't appear in any of the pictures, so I assumed she didn't join the boys on this little adventure. I scanned the photos more carefully. In some, Travis posed with them, and he appeared in the background in others. He was impossible to miss with that pink hair. There were a few of Lucien locking lips with a few women while his boyfriend – or whatever he was – looked on, his expression unreadable. What did he think of his lover's promiscuity?

How did it feel to live in such a body? To do whatever he wanted, to possess such freedom to be that liberal? Lucien might fool all of his followers, but he wasn't fooling me. Deep down, he was burying his pain in partying. It might have appeared so glamorous, but like me, he was relying on alcohol to bury the pain and to forget.

Chapter Nine

I opened the door of a Victorian pub that had a real fireplace, which made the atmosphere homey. The place wasn't busy, even though a band was playing on the stage. Ben was sitting at a table in the corner, sipping from a pint and dressed in a khaki jumper and jeans.

'It's nice to see you,' he said, smiling when I approached the table.

His peppery cologne filled my nostrils, and I sneezed.

'Bless you,' he said.

'Thank you.'

'What can I get you?'

I pushed the chair and untangled my scarf. 'Um… white wine, please.'

He nodded, stood and went to the bar to get the drinks while I got my bearings. I didn't have to be nervous. It was just a drink with a man. A man whom I sat across from in an interview room at the police station. Could detectives do that? Have drinks with an ex-witness? My hands were shaking, and I rubbed them together. Ben returned with my glass of wine, and I made a mental note to drink slowly.

He sat across from me. 'So, how are you?'

'I'm fine… I mean, trying to get past the whole experience. It was scary.'

'Trauma takes time to go away. Are you speaking to someone?'

I blinked. 'Someone?'

'Therapy?'

'Um… no… I….'

'It usually helps.'

I hadn't thought about speaking to a therapist. It was probably a good idea to talk to someone. I took a sip of wine and thought of topics to talk about with Ben. His job should be easy. I didn't think he would want to talk about it, but people liked to talk about themselves. Where had my social skills gone? The old me didn't have a hard time picking a conversation. That's how my life was divided – between the old me and the new me. I didn't like the new me, this creature that took my body.

'I'm sorry,' he said. 'I haven't done this in a while. I don't want you to think I'm throwing therapy on you.'

I smiled. 'I haven't thought that. You must have a few interesting stories to say, though, being a detective.'

'Well, in my job, I see many bad things happen to good people. You're in marketing, right? That must be interesting.'

'Not as interesting as yours, but it pays the bills.'

I talked about my job and felt more at ease. Ben told me he wanted to be a lawyer before he became a policeman.

'What field you would have picked if you were a lawyer?'

'Criminal law,' he replied.

A woman walked past our table dressed in a lovely velvet coat. Beside her was Asian man, but it was her purple hair that caught my attention. She wore black-and-white tights and Mary Janes. Was that Sasha? Her back was to me, so I couldn't make her out properly. Ben stood to get more drinks. I studied the woman carefully as her companion placed the order with the barman while she tapped on her phone. It *was* Sasha, and my stomach clenched. Of all the pubs she could have walked into, why this one in Highgate? Her eyes averted from her phone and looked straight at me, and I went cold. Her mouth parted as she saw me and looked at Lloyd, as if unsure what to do, then she said something to him.

Ben returned to the table and placed my glass of wine down with a thud, making me jump. Sasha and Lloyd moved away to a table at the far back and sat down, her back facing towards me, but I could see the blue glow of her phone. Was she alerting her friend that I was here having a drink with a man? Why should Lucien care when we had lost touch? Although there were many unsaid words between us, along with a mix of emotions. Lucien was the victim in all of this, as was I. He didn't choose what kind of family he was born into. Ben resumed the conversation on safe topics: favourite food, books, music, and holiday destinations. I engaged with him but kept my eye on Sasha. Not once did she look back.

Ben glanced over his shoulder. 'Do you know that couple?'

I gazed at him. Of course, he would pick up on it. The detective in him wouldn't be able to help it.

'No,' I fibbed.

Lloyd was looking at me now, and I saw Sasha's head turn slightly.

'It's getting late,' I said. 'I should go.'

'Okay,' he said. 'Do you want to do this again?'

'Sure.'

I stood, and Ben gave me a peck on the cheek but didn't offer to walk me home. I wasn't expecting him to, but it would have been nice if he had offered. Sasha looked at me as I put on my scarf. What was it with those kids? First Jan getting in touch with Anna after a year of silence and now randomly running into Sasha in a pub. Once upon a time, I had drinks and chatted with that girl as if we were best friends. Now it felt so weird, but I wasn't expecting her to come and greet me with hugs and kisses.

I breathed the cold air as I walked outside the pub. I wrapped the scarf tighter around my neck, and I could have been wrong, but it seemed there were faint sounds of footsteps behind me. I glanced over my shoulder. No one was there, and the street was empty. I resumed with my pacing, and it sounded again. I didn't look back this time as I hurried on. My heart raced against my chest as I felt for the keys in my pocket. I glanced over my shoulder as I approached the house, but I couldn't make out anything. Was someone following me? Once inside the house, I leaned against the door and took in a long breath.

My phone buzzed in my pocket, but I ignored it as I checked the windows. No one was out there. I bolted the windows, made sure the door was locked, and moved to the bedroom in the dark. Was someone out there watching me, but I couldn't see them? Who? The person who placed the rose? What did they want? I closed the bedroom door and sat on the bed checking my phone. It was Ben asking if I had arrived home okay. How thoughtful… but should I tell him I thought I was being followed? Was I being followed? Was it just my imagination? I went to the bathroom, removed my makeup, brushed my teeth and prepared for bed. As I lay in bed, I replied to Ben. My fingers hovered over the apps, and I hated myself for doing this – constantly peering, always watching. I typed Lucien's name again on Facebook and Instagram, but nothing came up. I tried again and again, but nothing came up. That was odd. Had he deleted all of his social media accounts?

Chapter Ten

All of them were gone: his Facebook profile, fan page, and Instagram account. The cord that still tied me to him was now gone, and I had lost him. There had to be several reasons why he deleted them. Lucien had a significant social following, and people might have asked many uncomfortable questions. Maybe he got banned for twenty-four hours for posting something that didn't agree with these accounts' policies, but his photos were always classy and tasteful. Or he got fed up with them. The last thought made my throat go dry. Or maybe he knew I was looking at his social accounts. How could he have known? Or was he going over his list of followers and saw that I was still following him, so he blocked me? I looked for Sasha's next, and her profile was gone, too. I looked for Jan next, but he was still there. I wasn't friends with him, but I could see a few of his posts. His Instagram was there, too. What did it all mean? What were they playing at? Jan made the last update eight hours ago that he was back in London. Did that mean Lucien was back on English soil? I wondered if Lloyd knew that Sasha and Lucien had slept together.

I prepared for a meeting I had with a restaurant manager by planning out the marketing strategy I would use, but my mind kept drifting and I couldn't focus. This was taking over my life once again, making me unable to move on. Someone sent me roses with thorns, but who had gone into my old house and was now following me?

I called Mrs. Parker to find out if there was any additional activity, and she was happy to hear from me.

'Why don't you come down for a cuppa?' she asked.

I could dash off for a few hours, have tea with my former neighbour and ask her face to face rather than on the phone. Then I could check the house to see if there were any more surprises.

#

The fall leaves flew by my feet before they scattered away with the chilly wind as I stared at my old house – this burden that the real estate company couldn't sell. I was stuck with a house nobody wanted, while it continued to haunt me. A house couldn't haunt me. The experience did, though. I wanted it gone, and for a horrible second, as I looked at it and it looked down at me, I thought about what it would be like to set it on fire and watch flames eat their way through it. I shook that thought away; I could go to prison for it. It wasn't the house that was doing this to me.

I checked the windows, but there were no roses in there. I located Agnes's house and rang the bell as I adjusted my blazer. Mrs. Parker didn't hesitate to show her disapproval at our last encounter, so I made myself presentable for this visit. She was a woman who went by the belief that no matter how many lemons life throws at you, there was no reason to look unkempt. Clothes could serve as a shield – an armour of sorts. They're a protective barrier and a disguise for your weaknesses and troubles. Agnes opened the door and beamed at me. She was wearing an apron on top of her blouse and grey skirt. Her hair was curled immaculately. I pictured her with her hair rollers before going to bed and carefully removing them in the morning.

'Emily dear,' she said. 'Come in, come in.'

I stepped inside and followed her to the narrow corridor to her living room. The TV was on *EastEnders*, but the volume was turned down low.

'Been watching it since it came out,' Agnes said.

'That is quite a commitment,' I said.

She gestured to the floral sofa. 'Sit, sit.'

She was overly fussy, a behaviour that reminded me of Amelia. She disappeared into the kitchen, and for a woman in her seventies, she always had high spirits, a smile on her face, and her movements were brisk and filled with energy. I was in my thirties, and she would give me a run for my money. I was grumpy and moody, and getting out of bed in the morning felt like a chore and a drag. Agnes Parker returned to the living room holding a tray with a teapot, matching cups, and a tin of biscuits. I attempted to stand to help her out, but she scolded me for being ridiculous. I sat back down feeling like a schoolgirl who just got a telling off by her teacher.

'So, how are you? You look nice,' she said, sitting beside me on the sofa.

Did I look that bad last time? No wonder Mrs. Mitchell shut the door. She must have thought I was a homeless person or a drunk.

'Thank you,' I said. 'Sorry for the other day when I came here. I was under a lot of stress and… couldn't get much sleep, and—'

'Don't mention it, dear. I understand. Are you eating?'

What an odd question. Although my appetite wasn't as bombastic as it used to be, now I eat like a bird. Agnes poured me the tea. My hands shook slightly, and I needed to get my shit together. I was falling apart little by little, but I had survived so much to mess it up. I would not let whoever was doing this ruin me.

'Yes, I am.'

She offered me a plate of shortbread biscuits. 'Here, take a biscuit.'

I took a biscuit, and the taste of sugar and butter exploded in my mouth. I took two more, as I discovered I was ravenous because I hadn't had breakfast that morning.

'Did you notice any activity in the house?' I asked.

'No, but Lucien was here.'

The biscuit caught in my wind pipe, and I exploded into a fit of violent coughs. Agnes's face paled as she got up, rushed to the kitchen, hurried back out and handed me a glass of water.

'Drink,' she barked.

I took a sip of water and felt the blood rush down my face as my chest went tight. I drained the glass of water and Agnes went back to the kitchen to fetch more.

'Maybe I shouldn't have been so abrupt when mentioning that boy,' she said after I started to recover.

I detected a slight hint of malice as she said 'that boy.' Mrs. Parker had never liked Lucien. To her, being tall, thin, having long hair, dressing in all black, and wearing silver jewellery was too strange. She described him as *macabre*, even though he was anything but.

'He was here?' I asked after recovering from my coughing fit.

'Yes, he was here yesterday. He came to talk to Olivia,' Mrs. Parker explained.

I blinked at her. 'Who is Olivia?'

She glanced at me as if I had been hiding under a rock. 'The Mitchells, the couple who had bought the house off him.'

'Oh,' I said. 'Right.'

She took a small sip of her tea. 'She let him in, and he came out thirty minutes later.'

I pictured Mrs. Parker sitting by the window with her knitting, watching the house with the yellow door and timing Lucien's stay. Who needed Facebook when you could do this?

'Did you speak to him?' I asked.

She took another biscuit. 'No, I don't know what he was doing here.'

I recalled Olivia with her blonde hair, green eyes and delicate but sharp features. Was she a relative of Lucien? From his mother's side, perhaps?

'I don't know why he had to do that to his hair,' Agnes said, interrupting my thoughts.

'Oh,' I said. 'You know how it is these days with the youths. So, you have noticed nothing strange in my house?'

I didn't want to sit there and discuss Lucien's decision to dye his hair lilac. His hair. His business.

She munched carefully on her biscuit. 'No. Any interested buyers yet?'

I shook my head. 'I haven't had any updates.'

I made a mental note to call the real estate company and find out what was happening. I wanted that house gone out of my life. After the chitchat about her children and my work, I stood to leave, and Mrs. Parker told me to drop back by soon. I didn't want this to become a habit. I dashed down the street as a cricket was singing, and the sun was hidden behind a bed of stubborn clouds. I walked past the house again, standing alone and empty.

I checked the windows again, but nothing seemed out of the ordinary.

'Emily! Emily!'

I glanced over my shoulder, scanning the area and wondering who might be calling me. At first, I thought Mrs. Parker was chasing me down the street because I had forgotten something, but it wasn't Mrs. Parker. The yellow door was wide open, and Olivia Mitchell was waving at me.

Chapter Eleven

Olivia had moved from the door and walked to the pavement as I crossed the road towards her. The sleek Mercedes was parked in the driveway, and I wondered what Mr. Mitchell did for a living. I glanced back, and I saw the curtain of Mrs. Parker's house move.

'Emily, hi,' Olivia said.

'Hi,' I said, beaming at her.

'I'm sorry for closing the door on you the other day like that. I thought….' She paused and glanced at the flowers, searching for the right word. 'I don't know what I thought, to be honest. You used to live across the road, you said?'

'Yes.'

'You asked me the other day if I noticed any activity at your house. There was a man the other day showing the house to a couple. I assume they were interested buyers, but apart from that, nothing seemed out of the ordinary.'

'Oh, right, thank you for telling me,' I said.

'Would you like to come in for a cup of tea?'

'Um….' I stalled.

'Not here, though,' she said quickly, scanning the street. 'How about you meet me tomorrow? There is a great coffee shop around the corner. Shall we say at noon?'

'Sure,' I said.

'Okay, perfect.' Olivia's eyes went to Mrs. Parker's house. 'She is so nosy. Practically lives by that window.'

I didn't have a reason to comment about this; I knew what Mrs. Parker was like.

'Anyway,' Olivia said. 'I'll see you tomorrow.'

She cast me a brilliant smile, revealing a set of white teeth, then turned and walked back to the house shutting the yellow door behind her. I was about to walk away when my stomach clenched. In her front yard was a rosebush… but the roses were pink.

#

Perhaps I was too quick to accept Olivia's offer. Why did she want me to have tea with her in a coffee shop when her house was perfectly suitable? What did she want to talk to me about? Why not at her home? What was she hiding there that she didn't want me to see? Maybe she didn't like the thought of me being there because she knew I had been there before and I was a stranger to her. I had been inside that house many times; I knew what it looked like. I even had been in one of the bedrooms. That image came to me: him lying on the bed, his hair floating off the edge of the bed, his long legs propped up on the headboard. I poured myself a glass of wine at the thought of what transpired afterward. I was way over my head.

My excuse was I couldn't help myself. The 'get out of jail free' card. A man has an affair with a perky assistant at his workplace, and he would say I couldn't help myself. Ed had said that to me. A cliché. But I couldn't help myself. I tried to resist, but for how long do you go on ignoring and talking yourself out of it? He was too young, and he was this and that. It was a pathetic attempt; Lucien knew I wasn't immune to his charms. If only I hadn't gone to that club after I found out Ed had cheated on me and found Lucien there. If only he'd ignored me, but he knew I wouldn't turn him away. Everyone smiled when something beautiful was presented to them. Why would I be any different? I was human, and I was vulnerable. If only none of this had happened, I might still live in the house, unaware that the woman before me had gone missing.

Mrs. Parker said she had seen Lucien just yesterday going to Olivia's house. Why? What could he possibly want from there? Did he forget something, perhaps? I doubted it. He might have used a realtor to sell the property, so what business did he have with her?

#

I was back at Greenwich the next day, in a café that Olivia had suggested. This café had recently opened; it wasn't here when I used to live there. The smell of coffee beans and baked goods filled the air. I took a sip of my coffee and looked at the window. Outside it was sunny, and a group of students walked past the window clutching onto their phones. I couldn't sleep again last night, with my thoughts tearing into my brain.

Olivia walked in, dressed in jeans, a purple sweater underneath her expensive coat, and a scarf draped loosely on her long, delicate neck. Her blonde hair was brushed, and she wore a touch of blusher on her cheeks as well as lip gloss. She looked polished and confident. She walked towards me, her heeled boots clicking on the café's parquet floors as she settled her tote bag on the empty chair.

'Lovely to see you,' she said as she sat across from me. 'All is well?'

I was taken aback by her formality. Usually, it was 'how are you?' or lately, 'how are you holding up?' As If I were holding onto an edge of a cliff.

'Good,' I lied, taking a sip of coffee. 'And you?'

'I'm good,' she said.

The waitress came forward to take Olivia's order.

'Green tea, please,' Olivia said to the waitress. 'And um….'

'Another black coffee,' I said.

The waitress nodded and walked off with our order.

'How are you finding the neighbourhood?' I asked.

'Oh, it's wonderful. The house needed work, but we're happy.'

'You had it renovated?' I asked.

'Well, the décor looked like something straight from an eighties catalogue. They weren't much into interior décor, Lucien's parents.'

My eyes narrowed at how easily his name slipped from her tongue.

'Do you know Lucien?' I blurted.

Olivia looked at me sharply. 'Yes, I do know him.'

I glanced towards the window where a woman was walking and typing furiously on her phone.

I looked back at her. 'I've heard he came over to your house the other day.'

Olivia studied me carefully. 'Mrs. Parker told you this?'

I didn't want Mrs. Parker to get involved, but I couldn't say no either. Olivia puffed, looking annoyed now. 'I wish she wouldn't stick her nose in other people's business,' she grumbled. 'I've never met anyone so intrusive. She's always knocking, inviting me over for tea.'

'She is a lonely old woman,' I said.

'Always asking questions for gossip. I assume she was by the window, looking out. Why are you friends with her?'

'Well….' My words vanished.

'I know what happened, and how you had a relationship with Lucien,' she said.

'I wouldn't call it—'

'It's none of my business,' she said cutting me off. 'I'm not fishing for gossip. Your affairs are your business. I only bought the house off him.'

The waitress arrived with Olivia's green tea and my black coffee. I handed the waitress my empty cup before she paced away.

'You bought the house directly from him?' I asked.

'Yes, and I made him a deal. My husband and I were separated, so I bought the house for myself. We reconciled six months ago.'

Still, she didn't tell me why he was at the house.

'I just inherited a sum of money,' Olivia went on, sipping her green tea. 'I own a cosmetics company, and Lucien is a model and photographer. So, I thought I could use him for photographs and as a model.'

Lucky Lucien not only sold off the house by charming an interested buyer with his good looks and charisma, but got a deal on a job. His mystery pulled people in. It was what made him alluring.

'Oh,' I said. 'A cosmetics company? That's nice.'

Olivia took another sip of her green tea. 'It's not as glamorous as it sounds, and I don't manage it as I used to, but everything has to be run by me.'

So, that was what Lucien came to the house to discuss? His contract?

'So, you hired him?' I asked.

'It goes without saying. The company we use for models always gets these gorgeous men who are masculine and Mediterranean-looking. I want to go for something very different, and he's a good fit for it.'

Wouldn't she conduct the meeting at her company in the boardroom rather than at the house? I got into my second cup of coffee, which was my fifth of the day.

'My husband works long hours,' Olivia explained.

'What does he do?' I asked.

'He's a cosmetic surgeon.'

'Oh wow,' I said.

Between her cosmetic company and her husband, a plastic surgeon, no wonder she looked fabulous. Why a house in Greenwich? They could afford a place more upmarket.

'I spend a lot of time alone in the house since I don't go to the company offices as I used to. That's why I asked you here for a coffee. You seem like a nice person,' Olivia said.

Did Lucien tell her that? I wondered if she told him I had knocked on her door looking worse for wear, demanding if she saw something strange happening at my old house. He must have thought that sounded like Emily – paranoid, suspicious and always causing drama. Did he tell her to be friendly with me?

'Thank you,' I said.

She fingered her scarf. 'Would you like to have dinner sometime?'

'Um….'

'Sorry, that was too forward, but I would like to remain in touch with you,' she said.

'Sure,' I said. 'Let me give you my email.'

Chapter Twelve

I could only stare in bewilderment as my heart rocked against my chest. It lay on my doormat: a single dark-red rose with thorns, but there was a slight alteration this time – there was a note. I didn't touch it, but called Ben right away. He sounded preoccupied when he picked up, as if I had disturbed him from an important case. He told me he'd be there as soon as he could. I sat on my front step as people strolled past me, casting doubtful looks as I waited. From time to time, I took backward glances at the rose as if it would vanish. Finally, after a painful forty-five minutes, a silver sedan pulled right in front of my house, and Ben came out buttoning up the jacket of his grey suit. He removed his sunglasses and gazed down at me.

'Are you all right? I rushed out as soon as I could,' he said.

I pointed a shaking finger at the doormat without saying a word. Ben moved to the door, inspecting the rose without touching it. I stood by his side, where he took a pen out of his inner jacket pocket and flipped the rose to read the typed message.

Not rose petals, but bloodstains lie on your path.

Ben glanced up at me. 'Is this the first time you got something like this?'

I shook my head. 'I got another one just last week. It's in the bin in the kitchen, and I got another in my old house.'

He took out a pair of gloves and an evidence bag, placed the rose in there, and stood once more. 'How do you know someone placed a rose at your old house?'

I bit into my bottom lip. 'An old neighbour called me and told me she saw a figure in my house. So, I went to check and saw a rose inside. When I went again in the morning, it was gone.'

'You didn't go into the house when you saw the rose?'

'No, I was too creeped out.'

'And from where did you see the rose?'

'From the window, from outside.'

He nodded, and I wondered if he should write any of this down. But he had pocketed the rose in the bag, so that was something.

'When was this?' he asked.

'A few days ago,' I said.

'May I see the other one?' he asked.

'Of course,' I said, putting the key in the lock.

As I was about to nip inside, Ben told me to wait and went inside himself. I glanced over my shoulder, focusing on the tree, but nothing seemed to be there. A teenager came out of a house from across the street, slammed the front door behind him and plodded down the street, typing on his phone without looking where he was going. *Young people and their phones*, I thought.

'All clear,' Ben called out.

I walked over and shut the door behind me. Ben stood with hands on his hips as I went to the kitchen. There were plates with crumbs on them, empty wine glasses, and empty bottles of wine standing by the bin. Heat rushed into my cheeks. Oh, what he must think. What a difference from the clean, organised house he walked into when he first came to ask me about Ed's disappearance, now to this shabby mess of a house. I was a different person back then. Yet now I was embarrassed. Was this what I had become? I pushed the bin peddle with my foot, found the rose that now was dying, and handed it to him. He inspected it and then pocketed it in a different bag.

'You notice anything suspicious in the neighbourhood?'

I shook my head. 'No.'

'And this is the first time someone left a note with a rose?'

'Yes.'

'Can you think of anyone who could do this to you?'

Lucien, Sasha, or Jan. Who else? But this was just a suspicion. I couldn't start dropping names to a detective without proof.

'No.'

He raised an eyebrow at me. 'A secret admirer perhaps?

'A secret... no,' I said. 'That message doesn't read like a love note.'

'Some people have a twisted sense of humour and can be practical jokers.'

'Did you come here to humour me?' I asked.

'I like you, Emily. It might sound silly since I don't know you that well.' His eyes swept through my kitchen. 'Apart from you being untidy and loving your liquor.'

'Look,' I said.

'I'm not judging you. We all have our issues.' He waved the evidence bag. 'I have had to carry much worse in bags like these. That messes you up.'

He turned to leave.

'Wait,' I said.

He turned facing me. 'I will look into this, and in the meantime, I suggest you install a security camera. Like those little spy cams. You can find them online. They are inexpensive, but they do the job, and go easy with the drinking.'

Chapter Thirteen

I ordered a spy cam online after Ben left, and it was set to arrive within a day. I got some work done with a glass of wine for company. I was annoyed at Ben. Who did he think he was? Telling me to go easy with the drinking? If I walked into someone else's kitchen and found empty bottles of wine standing by the bin waiting to be thrown out, I would think the same thing. Maybe I should seek help rather than use alcohol as a coping mechanism. I heard nothing more from Ben, but he wouldn't get in touch so soon. He had more prominent cases to solve, but when I ended up dead in a ditch somewhere, then he would take it seriously. Who would mourn for me if I got fished out of the Thames? My parents, no doubt. Anna would be devastated, but the list of people who would grieve for me was short. Mrs. Parker would gossip about how she knew me, how delightful I was, and the traumatic experience that left me slightly unhinged and paranoid. I texted Anna to ask her what she was up to. That was an hour ago, and still no word yet.

I rubbed my eyes with the back of my hands and stood from my desk, taking the wine glass with me for a refill. I opened the fridge. No more wine. *Great*. I glanced at the mess on the floor. When was the last time this house had a proper clean? I picked a plastic bag from the cupboard and placed the empty wine bottles inside, disgusted with myself that I drank that much. I left the bag by the door to deal with in the morning. There were clothes on the sofa, and dust had made itself at home on the furniture. The old me would have a heart attack seeing this. The only thing that looked neat was my desk.

I picked a playlist and I dusted, swept, cleaned the bathroom, washed the floors, and changed the sheets. An hour went by, and I sat on the sofa staring into space. The desire to have a drop was so immense I couldn't stop thinking about it. I reached for my phone and clicked on Facebook. Anna had checked in that she was in a bar in Soho. I went to the search function and typed his name. Still nothing. Where was he? Where could he be? I ran another search and stared at the screen as a clue presented itself.

#

The cold air seeped into my bones as I stepped inside the club. *Why do these places have to be so cold?* The club had old pipes on the wall and parquet floors, black velvet armchairs randomly scattered around, and chandeliers hanging from the ceiling. Neon green lights flashed on the dance floor, where the youngsters were dancing in weird twisting motions as house music pumped into the speakers making my ears burst. I didn't have a plan. I just showed up there without knowing what I'd face, and I was alone. It was better that way. If I had asked Anna, she would bombard me with questions, and given why I was there and whom I was to track down, it would make her uncomfortable. A man appeared by my side, and though he said something, I couldn't hear him over the loud music, and I wasn't interested in what he had to say anyway. I turned away from him and took a tour of the place, scanning the beautiful faces that came and went. *Maybe he left.* By the time I got ready and came here, he could have gone elsewhere. I sipped my drink as I made my rounds. The dance floor was so green the people looked like aliens. A machine came alive and spat out smoke. I walked through the doorway while gulping down my gin, tasting of happiness. Here the music changed, and I recognised the song.

'Addicted to Love' by Robert Palmer was playing, and it felt like I walked in a different place. The walls were bare, with old portraits adorning them, the ceiling was high with wood beams, and chandeliers dangled from the ceiling. I noticed the bar was decorated with old books as I ordered another double gin and tonic with a good-looking barman. No dance floor here, but a few people were dancing. They were too young to know this song, but anyone could have an ear for good music. The barman slid the glass my way and winked at me as I paid. I turned and moved around, unsure what I was doing. I turned my head to my left, where a girl was dancing provocatively, and the guys in the corner were leering at her. On the armchair leaned a beautifully dressed young man with long, glossy hair shaved at one side. He was smoking, and our eyes met from across the room.

Chapter Fourteen

Jan didn't seem surprised by my appearance, as if he was half expecting I would show up. I took another sip of the gin and tonic and walked towards him.

'Emily,' he said, and moved away from the armchair, towering over me.

Jan, draped in black vintage jewellery, looked like he had popped out of a genie bottle. He may have looked mesmerising and fabulous, but if he were a genie, this one wouldn't grant you any wishes.

He gestured to an armchair with his hand. 'If you would indulge me.'

I sat down. A girl carrying a tray whom I didn't notice before walked past, and he said something to her. She, too, stared at him as if he had just landed on a magic carpet, and I smiled as the girl hurried off with his order.

'What's so funny?' he asked, not sitting across from me so he could have complete control of the situation.

'You think you can do whatever you want, don't you?' I asked.

He shrugged and leaned forward, then placed his hands on the armchair. He smelled so strongly of cigarettes and cologne it made my head spin.

The girl reappeared by his side, eating him with her eyes, and he took the two glasses from her tray.

'Thank you, darling,' he said to her.

Turning several shades of pink, the girl moved away.

He handed me a drink. 'Why are you here, Emily?'

'I'm looking for Lucien,' I replied.

He gazed down at me, then sat down across from me. 'Why?'

I took a sip from the drink he bought me. It was too sweet. 'I want to speak to him.'

He fingered his hair. 'What about?'

'What are you, the gatekeeper?' I asked.

'I might as well be,' he said sharply. 'He's my best friend, and I have to protect him.'

'From what? From me?'

'Things haven't turned out so well for him since he set his eyes on you.'

'What happened to his mother wasn't my fault. If it weren't for me, he would still wonder where his brother is,' I pointed out.

He placed the glass down on the table and leaned closer, and his cologne wafted into my nostrils, making my head want to burst. 'Did you know Lucien was so devastated with what had happened he couldn't get out of bed for two months?'

I was taken aback by this. 'No, I didn't.'

'My point exactly,' Jan said. 'He has to see his parents in prison. Do you know how hard that is, especially to see his mother like that?'

'His mother killed three people, including my ex,' I reminded Jan.

He started fingering his hair again. 'I'm not saying his mother is a good person, but she is *his* mother.'

'Did he track down his biological father?'

He took a sip from his drink and licked his lips. 'I'm not going to answer that, and I shouldn't be telling you anything.'

'Yet you invited me to sit down with you and bought me a drink.'

'I don't see any reason to be rude.' He looked at me up and down. 'How is Anna?'

'She's fine. So, you're not going to tell me where he is?'

'They are living with me.'

'They?'

'Lucien and Travis, the bloke he's dating.'

'How delightful,' I said, taking another sip of the drink.

He smiled at me. 'What do you want from Lucien? He didn't get in touch with you for a reason. He wants nothing to do with you. You should have taken the hint by now.'

'I just want to talk.'

'He doesn't want to talk to you.'

'How do you know?'

He narrowed his eyes at me. 'You ruined his life, well… almost.'

'That's not fair,' I cried. 'I didn't do such a thing. If someone ruined his life, it was his parents!'

'His parents were shits, yes, but you shouldn't have gone sticking your nose where it didn't belong.'

'Tell him I want to speak to him. Can you do that?'

'I'll think about it.' He sighed. 'There is Travis to consider.'

'Travis has nothing to do with me.'

'Travis hates you for what you did to him.'

'Travis should mind his own business,' I said.

Jan smirked at this.

'Travis can come to find me and tell me whatever he has to say on my face,' I went on.

'I'm not a messenger, Emily. Now, shall we?'

I blinked at him. 'Shall we what?'

'Dance.'

'What?'

He rolled his eyes as if I were a massive weight on his shoulders. Then he stood and held out his hand to me. I drained my glass and took his hand.

'Attagirl,' he said.

'Would Anna get offended if she had to see you dancing with me right now?' Jan asked.

'Why should she?' I asked.

'Girls have a set of rules they follow.'

'And do you follow the rules?'

He laughed. 'Sometimes.'

'Would Lucien—'

'No, he won't. We don't have rules. He slept with Sasha, and their friendship is stronger than ever.'

'And have you slept with Sasha?'

'Yes.'

The way he said it so easily, as if he was telling me what he had for dinner, baffled me.

'Why did you stop replying to Anna's chats?'

'I see she told you,' he said with a smirk.

'Yes, she did.'

'I had a… crisis….'

'Why, after a year, did you reach out?'

'What is this?'

'You look after yours,' I said. 'And I look after mine.'

He smiled at this, and then the silence fell between us as he pulled me closer to him, and I could only stare, completely enamoured by this man as he backed away.

'I'm sorry,' he said apologetically, checking his watch, 'but I have to cut this short. I have another place to be.' He took my hand and kissed it, which threw me completely. It was so old-fashioned and courteous. Then he swaggered away saying nothing, leaving me staring at his back.

My evening wasn't entirely wasted. I found out that Lucien hates me, a motive enough for him to be doing this to me. Why hate me, though? I had set him free from the clutches of an obsessive mother who couldn't bear to see him with a woman, or anyone really. She wanted to keep him to herself, and Henry bullied him. But then again, I impeded a child's love towards his parents, because no matter what kind of people his parents were, they were all he had. So now he was alone, with nobody to care for him apart from his friends and his lover.

Chapter Fifteen

'You did *what?*' Anna cried.

'I'm sorry,' I said

I wasn't sure why I was apologising or why she was getting upset, and I hated the fact that she made me feel guilty. Did something happen between her and Jan? Had she met up with him and slept with him? But why would she lie about it to me, of all people?

'But why?' she asked. 'And how did you track Jan down?'

'Facebook,' I replied.

We were sitting outside a café in Leicester Square. People walked past us, all hurrying about their day as large cups of cappuccino sat in front of us. The sun was out, although grey clouds loomed overhead.

'Why?' she cried.

'I'm looking for Lucien.'

Anna buried her hands in her face. 'The obsession you have with that damn guy!'

I broke eye contact as a woman walked past, her heels clicking on the pavement and her phone pressed to her ear, telling the other person at the other end to fuck off. Each person who walked down these streets had their problems.

'Is this because of what happened? Is that what this is all about?' Anna asked.

I glanced at her. 'I want closure.'

'You had his parents arrested. There is no more closure for you.'

'But—'

Anna raised her hands to stop me. 'Emily, you need to let it go. Move on, get on with your life. Did you meet that hot detective for a drink, as I suggested?'

'Yes.'

'And?'

'And nothing….'

She rolled her eyes. 'For God's sake.'

'Why are you so upset about this? Did something happen between you and Jan? I tracked him down. We had a drink. I danced with him. That was it.'

'You stalked him, not tracked him down, and I know nothing happened.'

'Are you sure?'

'Of course, I am sure. I have to be there for something to happen now, don't I?' she retorted.

'Well, he is gorgeous,' I pointed out.

'So what? I rub shoulders with handsome men all the time. It doesn't mean I would jump into bed with every one of them.'

'But Jan is on another level.'

'Emily!' she snapped. 'Just because you couldn't help yourself and you were weak, it doesn't mean I am like you!'

I lowered my head as tears stung my eyes.

Anna sighed. 'I'm sorry, I was out of line. I didn't mean to be a bitch. I just want you to let him go. He has your number and you are friends on Facebook. If he wanted to talk to you, he would have by now. So, take the hint, Emily.'

Anna didn't know that someone was out there fucking with my head. She left shortly after our conversation to go back to work, but I lingered at the café for a little longer and ordered a chicken pie for lunch. After I finished my lunch, I ordered my first glass of wine of the day. I was trying to limit my drinking to four drinks a day. An image came to me when I saw Lucien for the first time after his parents were arrested. I went with my mother to the house to help me pack a few things. He was there by the window, and we looked at each other. Jan told me he couldn't get out of bed for two months after that. I mentally zoomed in on his face. I was always more focused on his glory instead of on what his face showed, but now as I thought about it, his hair was dry and coarse, the dark circles were visible under his eyes, and his skin had blemishes. Now, it seemed he had recovered. At least that was what his social media told me. He reconnected with his old flame, went to festivals, and still got offers for modelling jobs. Not all was lost. Another image came like a slap on the face: me, in my cabin on the cruise. I was in a cami top and underwear, downing the small liquor bottle from the minibar with tears in my eyes.

The waiter placed the yellowish glass of wine on the table, interrupting me from those images. As I picked up the glass and took a sip of wine, my toes curled with pleasure. A young man, more like a boy, sat six tables away from me, glaring. He had high cheekbones, a flawless complexion, a wide jaw, a full set of lips, and pink hair. Travis. I swallowed the saliva that had gathered in my mouth. For how long had he been sitting there watching me? Did he follow me? What did he want?

I knew what he wanted. Jan had told him to come and tell me whatever he had to say to my face. He stood from the chair and came towards my table, and we surveyed each other for a second or two, the boyfriend and me. What was I to Lucien? What was he to me? Travis didn't look older than twenty-four, and it went without saying he was exquisite-looking. It was like you had to go through a test to fit into that group. They reminded me of high school, and every school had that group, the popular ones whom everyone admired and idolised. And later, as years went by, you realised they were nothing special at all.

The number of hours they spent perfecting their look, picking what to wear to be overdressed but never over-elegant, putting on layers of masks, and the effort it took. Travis was wearing a blouse that I recognised, which belonged to Lucien –

black with vertical sheer stripes – and I also remembered most of the jewellery sponsored by our mutual friend. This boy wanted to be him, not be with him. He should focus on getting to know himself, not pretending to be someone he isn't.

'Why can't you leave Lucien alone?' he demanded.

I stared at him, not knowing what to say.

'Why are you doing this?' he asked.

'I just want to chat,' I said.

'It's not going to happen… not on my watch.'

'Don't worry,' I said. 'I'm not going to take him away.'

'I'm not worried about that, but I'm worried he will get hurt again,' Travis explained.

'So, I see the message came across,' I said.

'And don't stalk Jan in clubs,' he warned. 'It's not cool. Leave us the fuck alone,' he said and stomped off.

I glanced over my shoulder as I watched Travis plod down the street, running his hand over his immaculately styled hair. Jan said that he was sheltering the love birds. Little did this idiot know he just offered me an opportunity.

Chapter Sixteen

I stayed behind as much as possible but kept an eye on the pink head. He went down the stairs that led down to the tube, and the train screeched under the metal as Travis typed on his phone using both hands before he took the tube to the Northern Line. I took the second car and took a seat where I could see his pink head. Dying your hair in an extravagant colour wasn't a good idea if you wanted to blend in. It was too easy to spot, too distinct. He didn't stop scrolling and typing on his phone throughout the journey, then took the stop to Clapham. He stopped at a sushi place and came out a few minutes later with two bags loaded with food. I stayed behind, but he was too occupied with his phone to pay attention. Finally, he walked towards a block of glassed apartments that looked like a mini skyscraper. He punched in a code, and the door buzzed and clicked. Travis disappeared inside as the door shut behind him. I stood on the pavement staring at the block, and my heart did a little jog as I looked up at the balcony, spotting the blonde hair. Lucien, dressed in black, had his feet propped up on the table. I could see something was on the table, a bottle of beer maybe, and he was scrolling on his phone. As if in a trance, I watched him gracefully stand up and walk inside. My phone went off, making me prance, and I answered without looking to see who it was.

'Yes?' I said, my voice sounding clipped.

'It's Ben.'

'Oh, hi,' I said, looking up at the apartment, but I couldn't see anything anymore.

'I have looked at the roses.'

'Aha,' I said, taking the route back to the tube.

'These types of roses are called the Black Baccara, hence why the red is so deep, and in fact, is actually burgundy.'

'Okay,' I said.

According to the analysis, these types of flowers can be grown in any garden and are hybrid tea roses.'

'So, you think they are home grown, not from a store?' I asked.

I heard the ruffling of papers. 'They can be grown in a garden or found at a florist's shop,' Ben explained. 'It's hard to tell if they were bought in a store or cut from a garden. Can you think of anyone who grows these types of roses?'

Olivia had a rose bush, but hers were pink, unless she had another rose bush at the back. Mrs. Parker had flowers in her front yard, but nothing resembled roses, especially something as gorgeous as those.

'No,' I said.

'The lab got back to me regarding the fingerprints,' Ben explained. 'But there are none, and the ink used was an HP

LaserJet, which there are thousands. And the paper was plain, cheap paper, which everyone sells. So, it's dead end.'

'What do I do now?' I asked.

'Did you get the security camera installed?'

'It should be delivered this afternoon.'

'Good. If you get something like this again, let me know.'

Someone said something to him in the background. 'I've got to run.'

He clicked off before I could say anything else.

When I reached Highgate, I checked my phone. I had an email from Olivia asking me if I was free on Friday night. Her husband was working late and she suggested we have dinner at Pied-à-Terre. I sighed. She suggested a Michelin-starred restaurant in the city, overpriced and swanky, which meant I had to dress up, keep my alcohol intake at bay, and wipe out my chequebook. I could say I was sick, but when was the last time I went out?

The camera delivery arrived that afternoon. After reading the instructions manual, I set the camera up over my door. It was small, hardly noticeable, and I installed the app on my phone. I felt much more at ease, but the dread didn't seem to pass completely.

#

The taxi dropped me off at Charlotte Street in front of the restaurant. I was dressed in a fitted black top, a white high-waisted A-line skirt with colourful stripes, and pointy heels that made my feet complain. I made such an effort for this that I went to a hairdresser to have my hair trimmed, coloured and blow-dried, as it was long overdue. The white nail varnish on my nails looked like correction fluid.

Olivia was already there, dressed in a red designer suit and pointy white pumps that resembled mine, but hers were more expensive.

'Ah, Emily,' she greeted, giving me pecks on the cheek. 'You look gorgeous.'

'Oh, thank you,' I said.

'Thank you for joining me. I thought you might be busy on a Friday, a lovely young woman like yourself.'

'No, I had nothing planned.'

'No man?'

'No.'

'Oh, that's a shame. So, Mrs. Parker came around to my house again,' Olivia said with an eye roll.

'What did she want?' I asked.

'Can you guess?'

'To come over for tea?'

'If I knew she was that tedious, I wouldn't have bought the place. Even though he said she was unbearable, I did not know how much.'

I let Olivia do all the talking, and she told me she had been married for twenty years, was separated because her husband cheated on her with his assistant, but she gave him another chance. They had two daughters, Kylie and Fiona. Kylie lived in Switzerland, and Fiona graduated from art school last year and worked in a gallery as an assistant. Olivia ordered a five-course meal, and I did the same. She ordered an expensive bottle of red wine, and I mentally counted how much this dinner was going to cost me.

'You were engaged, right?' Olivia asked.

'No,' I said. 'Who told you that?'

She took a sip of wine. 'He did.'

Lucien knew I wasn't engaged. So why was he misinforming people and talking about me with Olivia?

'No, I wasn't,' I said. 'Ed, my ex-boyfriend, had bought me a ring, but I left him because he cheated, and then he went missing.'

'I'm sorry. I didn't mean to upset you. I tend to be blunt and not think before I speak,' Olivia said.

'Have you seen him?' I asked.

Olivia rose a perfectly arched eyebrow. 'Do you want to know?'

'Yes.'

She eyed me carefully. 'You're still in love with him, aren't you?'

I scowled at this as if it was the most absurd thing I had ever heard, and I took a sip of wine to buy myself time. I didn't know how to answer her question. Was I in love with Lucien? Olivia spoke again before I did, which was a relief.

'We did some test shots, but the lilac hair needs to go. It's not working. He has naturally platinum blonde hair, so why mess with it?'

'I don't know,' I replied.

'Kids these days,' she said.

The rest of the dinner went on smoothly. When the bill arrived, Olivia insisted she'd pay.

'Don't be ridiculous. I invited you,' she told me.

Next time, I had to pick up the check, and if I suggested a restaurant, it wouldn't be as grand. We walked outside the restaurant, and she gave me a peck on the cheek before she crossed the street. I hailed a taxi, and as I was about to tell the cabbie the address, I made out Olivia chatting with a young man with black hair. I pressed my face to the window as she threw her arms around him as if she hadn't seen him in years. That young man was Jan. What the hell was going on? How did she know Jan?

#

I was finally about to fall asleep when my phone buzzed on the bedside table. It was still dark out, and a dog was barking in the distance. It was Anna's father. I didn't know why he was calling me, but when I answered it, the room spun.

Chapter Seventeen

I rushed to the double doors and located the reception area with my heart in my mouth. The clerk told me I couldn't see her as I wasn't a relative, and as I was about to argue that her father had invited me, Mike, Anna's father, appeared looking pale, his face contoured with worry.

I rushed to him. 'Is she okay?'

Of course, she wasn't okay. Mike guided me to the coffee machine as he explained what had happened. Anna met a few work colleagues for drinks, which led to clubbing. Then she left the club with her colleagues and got a taxi, where one girl got into an argument with the driver for smoking in his cab. The driver, an Indian man, told her not to smoke, and she made racial comments when the driver asked them all to leave. Anna, worse for wear, got out of the taxi and told them she'd get another cab on her own as she didn't want to be associated with any of that nonsense. She dropped her bag on the ground, and when she went to pick it up, someone dragged her into a corner and assaulted her. Her nose was broken, and she was suffering from broken ribs. They were going to keep her in the hospital for a few days. A group of teenagers found her on the ground and called an ambulance and the police. This was all too much. I was still processing what I myself had seen – Olivia and Jan together, and how she flung her arms around him.

Were they having an affair? Was he an old friend? Had she hired him to model for her company? It felt strangely intimate to hug him like that. Maybe Lucien recommended Jan to her for another project? Still, something didn't feel right. Olivia bought the house from Lucien and hired him to model for her. But where did she fit in all of this? Now Anna had been attacked, and somehow, I felt it was all connected. Someone was out there plotting all of this, and now they went after my friend, which was unacceptable. This was getting bigger and far worse than before. Tears smeared down my face. *Poor Anna*, I thought, *how terrified must she have felt?* Mike put his hand on my shoulder as I cried quietly, and he passed me a tissue. It was all my fault. I had to fix it and find out who was doing this.

#

The weather was wretched, just like how I felt. Thunder clapped when I arrived back at the house, and rain hit the windows. I still hadn't seen Anna, but her father assured me he'd call me once visitors were allowed. I didn't want to stay alone, so I packed a pair of jeans, two sweaters, underwear and socks, and I went to my parents' house in Richmond. My mother's face went white when she saw me pale and teary-eyed.

'What's wrong?' She gasped and pulled me inside to the warmth.

I broke into tears when I smelled toast and freshly brewed coffee, which comforted me. My dad came to the door.

'What on earth—'

I rubbed my nose on the sleeve of my jacket. 'Anna has been attacked.'

My mum threw her hand to her mouth, and my dad's mouth gaped open.

'What?' he said.

Mum made me sit down with a cup of coffee and placed two slices of toast in front of me. I took the toast, smeared it with butter until it started to drip off, and took grateful bites. I felt guilty for having an appetite when my best friend was lying in the hospital with her face black and blue and in so much pain.

'How did this happen? When she was attacked?' my mum asked, sounding worried.

I told them what Anna's father had said to me.

'I must call him, the poor man,' my mum said after I finished relaying the story to her.

'Good idea, and I'll buy some flowers,' Dad said.

When Anna was ten, she lost her mother in a car crash, so it was just her and her dad, with whom she had a close relationship. I went up to my old bedroom with my mind churning, trying to come up with a plan. There was no proof that Lucien, Sasha, and Jan were doing this. I wanted to know what Olivia's business with Lucien and Jan was. I was starting to believe her relationship with them was more than professional.

Chapter Eighteen

Anna was propped up on the pillows, and I tried to disguise my shock when I saw her. She looked much worse than her father had described. Her right eye was swollen, the bruises on her face were black and blue, and there was a stitch above her eyebrow. Her nose was bandaged, and she looked away when I entered the room. Get well soon cards and flowers were on the bedside table.

'Darling,' I said to her as I placed the large bouquet of lilies on the bed.

'Emily,' she said in a hoarse voice that didn't sound like her.

I took a seat on the chair and took her hand.

'I feel so stupid, God.' She rubbed her forehead and winced.

'What did the police say?' I asked.

'They are looking into who could have done this.'

'And you don't recall what happened?'

'No, it was a blur. I didn't see his face, and I was drunk. The last thing I remember was leaving that taxi after the driver kicked us…' She attempted to reach for the glass of water.

I handed it to her and she sipped carefully with a straw.

'Fiona, my colleague, is an idiot, she couldn't handle her drinking, and she started snarling with the taxi driver for smoking. It was all so stupid.'

'But they left you behind when you got out of the taxi?' I asked in disbelief.

'I don't know… I remember I was pissed off at her, but you don't talk to people like that anyway… And then I woke up here in the hospital.'

'And you have no idea who would do this?' I asked.

'Some lunatic… The world is filled with them preying on women. I hate men.'

'So, you think a man did this?' I asked.

'No woman would do this to another woman.'

'And what did the police say?'

'They checked the CCTV at the club, but nobody looked suspicious.'

'I'm sorry,' I said.

'For what?'

'For everything, for going to that club, and—'

'No, I'm sorry, I shouldn't have lashed out at you like that…' She took more sips of water. 'The thing is, I wasn't completely honest with you.'

I waited for her to go on.

'I did… meet up with Jan.'

I stared at her with my mouth gaped open, fishlike.

'He texted me, and I agreed to meet him. He's so gorgeous it was hard not to… I couldn't believe that a guy like him would even give me the time of day. I met him in this club for drinks.

Everything was going well. Then the pretty girl with purple hair showed up, Sasha.'

'What happened?' I asked.

'It got strange after that. She's overly friendly in a way. I felt disarmed by her, but she took over and suggested we go to another club I had never heard of. So, I thought sure, I'll play along even though I wasn't exactly happy with her coming with us.'

'But Jan had invited her. Was she alone?'

'Yes.'

'Her boyfriend wasn't with her?'

'No, she had a fight with him and was pissed at him. She had told me she was… looking for a good time. I was wrong, however, it wasn't a club but an apartment where they took me. There were a few stoners nodding away in the corner, and we went to the other room, which was the bedroom.'

'Oh, Anna,' I said.

'It's not as you think. She took out this small vial of… cocaine, I think. She and Jan took a hit, but I didn't. I'm fine with booze, but I draw a line with drugs. Well, you know me. I'm not that person, so they started kissing and taking off their clothes, and I left then, annoyed that the evening turned out to be a complete waste of my time. I never spoke to him after that.'

'So, they started having sex in front of you?'

'Yes.'

I rubbed my forehead as if I had a headache. Lucien had slept with Sasha, and Sasha was sleeping with Jan, and she had a boyfriend, yet Jan said he slept with her only once. And when I asked about Anna, he said nothing about meeting her. Perhaps he was embarrassed.

'But she has a boyfriend,' I protested.

'As if that would stop certain people. I think she has the best of both worlds, the boyfriend and the beautiful friend who sometimes becomes her lover. And, from what I gathered, Jan has commitment issues.'

'Why didn't you tell me about this?'

Anna looked away. 'I was embarrassed.'

'You didn't have to be.'

'They are different from us. Friends or lovers are the same things to them. I admire them in a way.'

I took her hand again and squeezed it gently. 'Anna, do you think Jan did this to you?'

'*What*? Beat me up? No!' she exclaimed.

I rubbed her hand. 'Don't be so shocked.'

'No, I never saw him after that night, and why would he attack me?'

'I don't know, because you're my friend, and I had his best friend's parents arrested.'

'Then why didn't he come after you?'

'I don't know.'

#

I was so behind at work, I had to work day and night to keep up, but I had to get to the bottom of this. What if I couldn't, and this person kept on leaving roses on my doorstep and attacking the people I cared about? Then what? I typed Travis's username on Instagram: *mono_monstercookie*. There were several pictures of him with his friends and a few with Lucien, which had the most likes and comments. The last photo he uploaded was a selfie dated two weeks ago.

I put the phone away and went down the steps to the tube, and a man overtook me, skipping down the stairs. A rumble of thunder clapped, and rain poured. I entered the cafe at the tube station and ordered myself a macchiato. I found a free table by the wall, and with my back facing the other commuters who were buying their coffee to go, I opened the cup lid, looked over my shoulder, and then poured gin in my coffee. My train was due to arrive any second. I flung my handbag on my shoulder and collided with someone, and hot coffee went flying, splashing all over my jeans and on the other person's torso. There was swearing from the other party. I looked up, ready to utter my apologies, and my mouth gaped open as her black-rimmed eyes bore into mine. Sasha.

Chapter Nineteen

Sasha wasn't happy as her white vintage blouse was stained with coffee. Her purple hair was curled with a curling iron, and a bow sat prettily on her head. She wore dark lipstick, the colour of the roses I had been getting.

'You,' I said.

'For fuck's sake, Emily,' she barked. 'Watch where you're going. This is an expensive blouse, and you ruined it. And what is that smell? Is that gin? Seriously, you need to get a grip. You're such a loser.'

Whatever happened to the chatty, bubbly girl I met at the club who kept asking me to try on the dress she had designed?

'There is no need to get verbally abusive. It was an accident,' I retorted. 'And you should watch where you're going.'

'You like to ruin things, don't you?'

'Look, I'm sorry,' I said. 'Are you hurt?'

She lowered her head and broke into tears. Commuters looked at her, then at me, and continued with their day. I ushered her into the café and made her sit on one of the long stools while I ordered another macchiato, no gin now since the last drop got wasted all over Sasha's blouse, and a tea for her. I went to the table and placed the cup in front of her. Mascara was smeared all over her otherwise immaculately made-up face. I handed her a tissue, and she yanked it from my hand with polished pink claws and dipped it under her eyes. She was going to have a story to tell her friends.

Why did they keep blaming me for what happened to Lucien, though? I wasn't the one who killed Henry's mistress and made his brother's accident look like he had gone missing. They seemed to forget an essential factor: Ed was dead at the hands of Lucien's mother, too. Ed might have been shit, but he didn't deserve that. He was, in the end, the man I had a relationship with for four years. I didn't ask for any of this. I sat across from her and took a sip of my coffee while she got her bearings. The smell of coffee beans wafted in the air, and the smell of bread made my stomach grumble, reminding me I hadn't eaten anything yet. She peered at me beneath her fake eyelashes.

'I'm sorry,' she said. 'I shouldn't have lashed out at you like that.'

She seemed to be returning to her usual bubbly self, which took me aback by how her mood had shifted suddenly.

'What were you doing in that pub the other day?' I asked her.

She took a sip of her tea. 'What do people do at pubs?'

'It doesn't seem your kind of pub.'

'Lloyd likes that pub, so we went there. Is there an issue?'

'No issue, it's just that….' I sighed. 'Never mind.'

'The guy you were with, isn't that the detective?'

'How do you know him?'

'Well, we had to go to the station and answer questions when it all blew up. He's cute, though. You have good taste…' She paused a beat, then, 'Of course, you do.'

'What is that supposed to mean?' I asked.

'Nothing, just that you have good tastes. How is Anna?'

'Anna?' I asked.

Did Sasha know about what happened? Did it make it to the news? The last time I checked, there wasn't anything, and most cases aren't reported in the news.

'Yes,' she said.

'Why are you asking?' I asked.

Her eyes lingered on me. 'Nothing. I'm asking because…'

Because Sasha had crashed Anna's date with Jan even though Sasha already had a boyfriend.

'Did she tell you? About her date with Jan?' she asked.

'Yes, she did.'

'She got weird at the end and left.'

I took a sip of my coffee. 'Can't say I blame her.'

'It was harmless fun. She could have joined if she wanted to.'

'Anna is not that sort of person.'

'What sort of person is she? She doesn't seem like the type who's prudish, but I was wrong.'

'With all due respect,' I said, 'but you have a boyfriend.'

She shrugged. 'We have an open relationship.'

I glanced at the window where people were passing by, hurrying to get to some place. 'I see.'

'Aren't you going to ask me?' she said in a small voice.

I glanced at her. 'Ask you what?'

She looked at me sharply. 'About him.'

The screeching of trains hissed into my ears.

'Sometimes,' Sasha went on, 'I catch him staring at the window in wonder. I think he misses you.'

'Sasha, let's not get into this,' I said.

'It's a red zone, I know. He was so sad after what had happened. His parents are odd, but I had no idea how much, especially his mum. I had no idea she's insane.'

'Did you tell him that his mother is insane?' I asked.

Sasha shook her head. 'I don't need to. He knows.'

I fingered my cup. 'Does he go to visit them in prison?'

She took a sip of her tea. 'Yes, twice a week, well, his mum.'

I looked up. 'What about Henry?'

'Henry doesn't want anything to do with him.'

'Oh,' I said.

'He told him he had one son, and he was dead.'

'That is… awful.'

'It is,' she agreed and checked her phone. 'I have to go. I need to get myself a new blouse, and I'm already late.' She stood. 'Thanks for the tea.'

She was about to leave when I thought of something and called out her name, and she turned back to face me.

'Can you not tell Lucien about us running into each other.'

'I wasn't planning to,' she said.

#

It was late evening when I arrived at the house to check on a few things. The sky was dark, and lamps cast their soft glow as the chill of the night air settled into my bones. With shaking hands, I fiddled with the key and somehow managed to unlock the door. All I wanted was to rush inside and pour myself a glass of wine. If I had any wine left. A car roared by, and I got that instinct that someone was not far away. Watching me. The fear leapt into me, crashing my insides. What if someone attacked me, too? Too many weird things were happening, and dread curled into my stomach. It took every ounce in me to turn around, and I screamed.

Chapter Twenty

He stood on the pavement in his uniform of black and leather. His long, lilac hair fell on his chest as he peered at me with his large, green eyes. A light went on from the house next door, and the window opened. It was my next-door neighbour, Mr. Stevens.

'Who screamed?' he asked.

I looked up, and Lucien didn't move, eyeing me with suspicion as if I were an unknown entity he had discovered.

'It's fine,' I said to Mr. Stevens. 'I didn't mean to alarm you.'

With a shake of the head, Mr. Stevens closed the window, went inside and turned off the lights.

My heart felt like it was going to explode as my mind swirled with a mix of emotions. He didn't yet say a word, but how did he know where I lived? Had he been watching me as I was watching him? The alarm electrified my senses. He looked away, then took a step forward, and I took a step back.

'Stay where you are,' I said.

'There is no reason for you to get dramatic,' he said.

'How did you find me?' I asked.

He raised an eyebrow. 'Really, Emily?

He was towering over me, and his eyes were on me like lasers. My bag slipped from my hand and dropped with a thud on the ground. The sound of my small glass bottles pierced through the air. He picked up my bag, and the bottles jiggled inside my bag as he furrowed his eyebrows. Then he gazed at me as if to say, *Oh, Emily*. He took the keys from my hand and went to my front door.

'Hey! You can't just—'

He looked at me over his shoulder and said, 'It's only me, Emily.'

There was the click of the lock as he pulled the door open, but he didn't go in. Instead, he pushed it with the back of his hand and stepped aside for me to go in first.

#

I held my breath as he sat across from me in my living room. Lucien on the sofa, me on the armchair that I bought from a boot sale. His long fingers twirled elegantly in his hair. He had rings on every finger, so beautifully adorned in silver and steel. He should be in a museum where people could stand in awe and admire him. I stood at once, almost knocking the chair over, and dragged myself in the kitchen, unable to contain it any more. I opened the fridge, but I had no wine left. *Fantastic*. I opened cupboards looking for something that contained alcohol. I wouldn't be able to go through with it, having him there in my house, without having at least a drop. Another flashback came to me. I was on the boat, in my cabin, while my parents slept next door, and I was having a party for one. I had bought a bottle of wine from the bar, and I paid for it in cash. I didn't want to leave any traces of my little misdemeanours. How often I washed my mouth with mouthwash and chewed on gum, how my body pinched and itched for that drop, to have that release. To let go and to forget. I found an old whiskey bottle in one the cupboards and poured it in a glass. I returned to the living room, where Lucien was scrolling on his phone. *Seriously,* I thought? What was wrong with this picture?

'Why are you here?' I asked.

He looked up at me. 'Sit down, Emily. We need to talk.'

'Oh, now you want to talk after a year of silence?'

He glared at me. 'I was angry at you.'

'Why? I haven't killed anyone.'

I took a gulp and savoured the burn it gave me.

He leaned forward. 'How much are you drinking?'

'Let's get into why you're here,' I said, ignoring his question.

He sighed and leaned back in the chair. 'As I said, I was angry… This hasn't been easy for me. My mum…' His words vanished. 'Can I have a drink?'

I went to the kitchen and brought the bottle to the living room, along with an empty glass. I handed the bottle to him; he took it from my hand and poured whiskey into the glass. He took long, grateful sips and licked his lips.

'She would have killed you,' he said.

'Then can you explain why you're so fucking pissed off?' I shouted.

'I was looking for someone to blame.'

'Blame your parents, not me.'

'My life fell apart after that. I was in shock. My new reality is visiting my mum in… prison.'

'Had you tried to tracked down your father. Not Henry, your—'

'I know what you mean,' he barked. 'No, I don't want to know.'

'But—'

'I'm not going to discuss this with you,' he said with fire in his eyes.

'And why now? Why, after a year, did you come to find me?'

A smile curved into his lips, but he didn't look at me. 'You always lurked in the back of my head.'

'What are you trying to say? That you miss me?'

He fingered his hair. 'Maybe.'

'But you have a boyfriend.'

'I do.'

I stood from the chair and went to the window, crossing my hands across my chest. I made out a couple playing Twister in the living room across the street. The woman threw her head back and laughed hysterically as she and her partner collapsed on the floor. I smiled and turned away from the window as I ran my hand through my hair.

'I thought Travis was done with you,' I said.

'We reconciled six months ago…'

I lowered my head. 'I see.'

Lucien was glancing back at me. 'Why don't you come and sit right next to me?'

'Does Travis know you're here?' I asked.

'No,' Lucien replied.

'Where does he think you are right now?'

'Does it really matter? I have Travis under control.'

I flumped down on the chair. 'Of course, you do. I bet you have him wrapped around your little finger.'

He threw me an ugly glare but didn't respond.

'Did Jan tell you I tracked him down?' I asked.

'No.'

'But you knew about it?'

'I heard him and Travis talk when they thought I was asleep,' he said.

Was that bitterness I detected in his tone? I imagined Lucien wasn't all too thrilled about this, to be discussed behind his friend's and lover's backs. That they were keeping secrets from him. Was that what I was? A secret. But who are we without secrets?

'Why are you stalking my friends?' he asked.

'I wasn't stalking… I was looking for you.'

'Why?'

I wasn't ready to tell him what was going on. I had to establish if he was doing this to me, but I doubted it. What did he have to gain from all of this? *Revenge,* that tiny voice in the back of my head reminded me.

'I don't like how things ended. What had happened was….' I trailed off.

'I wasn't thrilled either… but….' He sighed. 'It was a confusing time. I don't think I can get over what happened.'

'I know,' I said. 'How did you find me?'

'Everyone is findable. How is Anna?' he asked.

I stared at him. It was the second time I was asked this question. A chill went through me like someone had opened a window. First Sasha asking about Anna, and now him. Why were they invested in my friend's welfare?

'Why do you ask?' I asked.

'I'm simply asking how she is,' he replied, checking his phone. 'It's getting late. Travis will probably be wondering where I am. Can we do this again?'

'Yes, but give me a heads up. I don't want you to creep up on me.'

He smiled and stood. 'Whatever you say, Emily.'

I stood.

'Don't stand on my behalf. I'll show myself out.'

He walked to the door.

'Oh, and Lucien,' I said.

He turned right away. 'Yep.'

'Why did you dye your hair lilac?'

'That is your question? I wanted a change. Don't you like it?'

'No,' I said.

'Good,' he replied, and he left.

As he was leaving, I noticed there was a slight alteration to his distinct appearance. He always wore an onyx pendant with a silver chain that his mother had given him and Sylvian, but now the pendant was gone.

Chapter Twenty-one

I got another email from Olivia asking if we could meet up soon, and she suggested lunch at the Ivy. *All these expensive places to have lunch,* I thought. *Can't we just go to the pub?* I couldn't, however, picture a woman as sophisticated as her in a local pub. Since it was my turn to pay, and I wouldn't be able to afford that place, I suggested a pub anyway since it was not far from her house. In the meantime, I tried to catch up with work. I had three meetings lined up that week, and I was so behind I was considering hiring more help. I kept myself busy to avoid thinking of the stiff encounter with Lucien. *Encounter* wasn't the right way to describe it. I kept glancing at the sofa where he sat. The glass he had drunk from was still on the coffee table, and so was the whiskey bottle. I made a mental note to buy groceries and clean the house. I stood and went to the window and opened the curtain an inch – nothing unusual. Just cars rumbling by and an odd neighbour here and there. I shut the curtain and moved away from the window, facing the coffee table. My phone buzzed as I poured whiskey into the glass and drank from the same spot Lucien had drunk from. I went back to my desk and resumed my work.

Twilight was seeping from behind the curtains when I looked up from the screen. I had been working for hours and rubbed my tired eyes with the back of my hands. I checked my emails and found where Olivia had replied and said the pub would do OK. She suggested Saturday afternoon. I had nothing planned that day, apart from work. I checked my phone while trying to gather something to eat. I had three messages – one from my parents, and the others from Ben and Lucien. I stared at the screen as their names were on top of each other. Two men who couldn't be more different. One who was handsome, wore suits and was a policeman; the other was ridiculously beautiful, always wore black and was a model with a past.

I boiled the kettle to make Ramen, and my mind went back to Lucien. A year of silence, and now he re-emerged into my life. Why now? Was this part of some elaborate plan? I read Ben's text in which he told me he had heard about Anna being attacked, asked why I hadn't said anything about it and wondered if I could meet him at the pub tomorrow evening. I sighed and went to Lucien's text next. The text was long and the words blurred. I left the phone on the counter, backed myself away from it as if it were a medical complaint and then ate my dinner on the sofa in silence while trying to collect my thoughts. Something strange was going on, that much was clear. Someone was sending me roses, going into my old house, following me and going after the people I cared about, and it was all connected to Lucien, at least that's what I suspected. Maybe it wasn't him doing this to me, but someone was. Someone who knew him.

After I finished my dinner, I poured myself another glass of whiskey and built up enough courage to read Lucien's text. I pictured him sitting alone in Jan's apartment while the others were at work as he slowly composed the text, thinking of the right words.

Emily,

Things have become strained and weird between us, and I hate it. I did partly blame you for what happened. The truth is, my life has been shitty since I stopped speaking to you. I'm sorry for springing this on you now, as you have your issues to deal with and I have mine. I thought I would be fine and could carry on as I was and move on from it, but the truth is, I miss you a lot. I know this won't change things, but I had to put it out there.

L xxx

'For fuck's sake!' I said to the empty kitchen.

I didn't have time for his sloppy feelings. What was wrong with him? I took a sip of whiskey and then grimaced and poured it down in the sink. I stepped away from the phone to avoid typing a reply and went back to work. Why now? I kept pausing every five minutes, unable to contain my focus, and kept throwing glances at the kitchen where the phone lay on the counter, as if somehow it would move.

#

At ten o' clock at night, I strolled past Hyde Park as I breathed in the cold air and shoved my hands in my pockets, scanning the area. I had to find out what was going on, and he was the key. He was standing by the gate, waiting, the blue glow of his phone reflected on his pale face. He wore a black coat and a hoodie over his head. I thought how plush and expensive he looked, rather than like someone who was going through a shitty time. He looked glamorous, but people put on a lot of masks to disguise what was truly going on in their lives. Some chose to hit the bottle like me. Others wore an armour of clothes. I plodded towards him with my hands curled into fists. I looked up at him and noticed how long his eyelashes were. Were they that long before? Or had he done something to them? His face looked different – more angular and sharper. There was no other way to describe it, but he still had the same hypnotising effect on me. I came here so blindly to find out what the hell was going on, but also so unaware of how he could suck me back in.

'There you are,' he said.

'Have you been waiting long?' I asked.

'No.'

'That text…'

'I wasn't expecting a reply.'

'Why here?'

He rose his eyebrow. 'Do you have another place in mind? Your house, maybe?'

'Don't be silly,' I said, and walked away from him.

He kept up with me, and I turned to him. 'Does Travis know you're meeting me?'

'Why are you so invested in my relationship with Travis?'

'I don't want to get in the middle,' I argued.

'Leave Travis to me,' he said. 'Besides, there is no reason for him to get upset.'

'Why wouldn't he?' I asked.

Lucien sighed as if this conversation was boring to him.

'We have an open relation—'

'For Christ's sake,' I snapped. 'What is it with you people?'

They were in an open relationship, yet Travis went through all the trouble of tracking me down to tell me to stay away. Why do that if they were allowed to meet with other people? Perhaps Travis imposed a rule on him – anyone in the country apart from me. Why? What was Travis afraid of if they both slept around?

He looked at me accusingly. 'What?'

'This open relationship crap. Either you're exclusive or you're not.'

'We see things differently, and not everything is black and white.'

'Yes, it is,' I said. 'It's either you want to commit or not. It's simple. Don't waste the other person's time if you want to sleep around.'

He rolled his eyes. 'We both agreed. He's out right now doing whatever….'

'He came to find me,' I blurted.

Chapter Twenty-two

Lucien kept up with me again and grabbed me by the arm.

'Who came to you?'

'Travis.'

'*What?*'

'Judging from your reaction, he didn't tell you about any of this?' I said.

He let go of my arm. 'No, he didn't. What did he tell you?'

I ran my fingers through my hair. 'He told me to stay away from you.'

Lucien's eyes widened. 'He said *what?*'

'That's what he said,' I said.

Lucien rubbed his face. 'I'm sorry, I had no idea he… Goddamn it. Why did he do that?'

'Maybe he feels threatened.'

Threatened because Lucien might still have feelings for me. This thought morphed itself with alarm and fear.

'What?' I asked.

I lifted my hands and dropped them to my side. 'I don't know. I would appreciate it if you didn't tell him about this. He would know we spoke, and I don't want to get in the middle of a lover's tiff.' I turned and walked away from him. 'I have enough on my plate as it is.'

'Where are you going?' he called out.

'Looking for a pub,' I shouted.

Lucien grabbed my arm and crossed the street. He kept me like that, huddled into him as we walked in the cold. His boots thumped against the pavement, and I smelt fresh linen, hair products and perfume. Not a hint of sweat – always clean smelling while his mother smelt of butter and sugar. He turned corners, and at one point, my foot caught with his and I nearly tripped, but he held me in place. He walked fast, as if afraid of being followed, and my muscles went tense with this thought. He kept holding my arm as he turned another corner, approached a metal door, and pounded on it. It was like those doors seen in secret clubs, where part of it slides and just the eyes appear from the other end. Arabic music played as we descended the steps, and I could feel the warm air the further we walked. There were round tables with red tablecloths and small lamps. There was a small bar in the corner, and a pink-glowing stage where women in belly dancing costumes danced. I never knew such places existed, and I wouldn't be able to spot them. This news of Travis tracking me down had upset Lucien.

He found an empty table in the corner in the dark and made me sit down before he sat beside me. I watched the women on the stage swinging their hips, looking exotic and sensual, and someone approached our table. I looked up as a girl with a tray stood staring at Lucien. He ordered a beer for him and a diet

Coke for me. I was about to protest, but his icy eyes sliced to me and he said, 'You've had enough.'

'Who are you? My father?' I argued.

'You've had enough,' he repeated.

After the waitress walked off with our order, he turned to me.

'Walk me through what happened with Travis.'

'I already told you,' I said. 'Just don't tell him.'

'I won't, but I can't believe he did that.'

'Did you tell him about… us?' I asked.

He cast me a sideways glance. 'Yes.'

'I see,' I said.

We watched the dancers for a while. Then, the waitress brought his beer and my diet Coke.

'What did you tell him, if I may ask?' I asked.

Another sideways glance. 'He was suspicious when I invited you to the club.'

'Were you serious with him then?'

'No.'

'Why was he suspicious?'

'Because… well… I think he could sense that I was attracted to you.'

It made sense why Travis didn't introduce himself that night, and how he walked off and went to the dance floor.

'And you weren't upset about his departure,' I pointed out.

'He did it all the time. I was used to it by then. When we reconciled, I didn't mention you or anything like that. Then, one afternoon, he told me that I can talk to him about you and that I don't have to hide it from him.'

'And so you told him?' I asked.

'Not right away.'

'There wasn't much to say?'

He glanced at me. 'I think there was plenty to say.'

I took a sip of Coke, and he did the same with his beer.

'I'm sorry,' he said while glancing at the dancers, 'for everything that happened, what I put you through. It was selfish of me to blame you. My parents were such shits.'

'They are your parents.'

'Yeah, well… they sure fuck us up,' he said.

His attention averted back to the dancers. 'My dad wants nothing to do with me.'

I tried to feign surprise as Sasha had already told me this, and it seemed she had kept her promise and told him nothing of our encounter. If she had, he gave nothing away. He glanced at me, and there was a sad glint in his eyes.

'I don't understand why couldn't he love me. I'm not his by blood, but he is the father I know.'

I gazed down at his hand placed on the table, and I put my hand to his, his eyes going wide.

'Don't take it the wrong way, but don't you think it is for the best?' I asked.

He blinked at me but said nothing.

'From what you told me and what I have seen, he wasn't exactly nice to you,' I added.

'Have seen? What did you see?' he asked.

'I saw him push you. He was abusive, and one time…'

He kept staring at me. 'Go on.'

I sighed and stared down at my empty glass of Coke, and he signalled the waitress for another round.

'Please just let me have one drink,' I begged.

'Fine, just the one,' he said and placed an order for a glass of wine with the waitress.

'You were saying,' he prompted after the waitress had walked off.

'I was going to go over to your house, and I heard your parents… arguing. Then, he called you a… forgive me… a faggot.' I grimaced.

'He called me worse than that, but—he is my dad.'

When I lived in my old house, Henry had come over more than once yelling at me to stay away from his son. At first, I thought he didn't want me to talk to his son because Lucien was promiscuous and an exhibitionist, so open about his sexuality, and that I was older than him. Still, as it turned out, it had nothing to do with that. Instead, he was trying to warn me about his wife. I thought of the house in Exeter, where Lucien went every year on the anniversary his brother's disappearance, and I wondered if he kept going over there. Then I remembered Mrs. Parker told me he had sold off all the properties.

'Did you sell the house in Exeter?' I asked.

Lucien fingered the beer bottle. 'Yes. Now a nice family with two children lives there. At least I had closure. I can take comfort in knowing what happened to my brother.'

My heart went out to him. 'I'm so sorry.'

He gave me a sad smile. 'It's not your fault. If only I had woken up that night… If I had done something differently and stopped him from going out. If I hadn't gotten sick. If only—'

I squeezed his hand. 'There is no point in dwelling on the what-ifs. It's over now.'

He sniffed. 'But that doesn't mean I don't think about him.'

'It's okay to think about him. He's your brother, and you loved him.'

He leaned his back in the chair. 'I wonder what life would have been like if he were still alive. What he would be now. He would be twenty-nine, yet he will remain eighteen. Frozen in time. While I will get old.'

His parents had robbed so much from him – to hide such a shocking secret and to make him believe that his brother was missing when he wasn't. I would never comprehend what Lucien had felt. That level of hurt and betrayal. To have that shock that could never be replaced. Something like that would never leave a person. It would continue to haunt them. I wanted to ask him why he didn't wear the pendent any more, but it was too soon after reconnecting to ask, and he would tell me in his own time.

Chapter Twenty-three

After a meeting with two clients, I went to the hospital to visit Anna. She would be released in a few days but would stay with her father for the time being. Afterward, I took the tube back to Highgate. I didn't go home, but to a pub on North Road. My heeled boots clicked on the pavement as the sun was setting and music was coming from somewhere. I pushed open the pub door that had sixteenth-century décor. Ben was sitting at one of the tables with sofas, and he stood to greet me when I approached.

'Can I get you anything to drink?' he asked after the formalities were out of the way.

'I'll have a Coke,' I said.

He seemed surprised by this, but he went to the bar. I had to get my shit in order, and starting with keeping my drinking at bay was an excellent place to start. I watched him at the bar ordering drinks, then I checked my phone. There was a text from Lucien. I sighed. This was becoming a habit. Ben returned with our drinks and slid next to me.

'How did you know what had happened to Anna?' I asked him.

He narrowed his blue eyes at me. 'I'm a policeman. It's my job to know.'

'But aren't you, like, in different sections?' I asked.

'Policemen talk to one another. Why didn't you tell me about it?'

'I… I don't know… it's her you have to talk to, not me. I wasn't there.'

'I already spoke to her,' he said.

I gaped at him, yet Anna had mentioned nothing about this visit.

'It's my job to go around and ask people questions,' he added.

'You mean to see who is lying to your face?' I asked.

He took a sip of beer. 'That's one way to put it.'

I leaned forward. 'Do you like what you do? You surround yourself with awful things all the time.'

'I enjoy it because I put criminals where they belong, in prison, and I like to help people.'

'What did Anna tell you?' I asked.

'You know I can't disclose that information.'

I leaned my back on the sofa. 'Did she tell you what happened?'

'Yes, but she doesn't recall much,' he said.

I glanced over at a couple. The man was holding the woman's hand, and the woman was crying. Sadness plunged into me, wondering what kind of news the man had delivered to her. That he was breaking up with her? Had something happened to a loved one? Ben's eyes followed to where I was looking, and the woman grabbed her bag and walked out of the pub as the man stared at the stained glass.

I turned my attention back to Ben. 'Have you found anything else about the roses?'

'That's why I asked you to meet me here.'

Was that the real reason? When a phone call could have done the job?

'What did you find?' I asked.

'The roses are home grown.'

'How do you know?'

'It's my job to find this information. Those roses grow from late spring till autumn, and they don't like cold weather. I spoke to an expert who grows these kinds of roses, and she said their meaning is true love, hope and optimism, and mystery.'

'Are you trying to tell me that whoever is leaving me those roses is trying to deliver a positive message? That this is a declaration of love? Is that what you're trying to tell me?' I asked.

'I'm not saying that. The expert explained that roses are flowers of love, but this particular rose, because of its deep shade, the mystery part reflects its unnatural aspect. Black roses are not natural.'

'But the roses are not black. They're burgundy,' I pointed out.

'It's referred to as black,' Ben said.

Not rose petals, but bloodstains lie on your path, the message had said.

All of those terms, the black roses, and the message… it's something Lucien would do since he was into Gothic literature and dark romance. A chill ran down my spine; the roses had stopped now that he had reconnected.

'Are you all right?' Ben asked, snapping me out of my thoughts.

'I'm fine,' I said, reaching for the menu. 'I'm hungry. You want to order something?'

'Sure,' he said.

I scanned the menu, yet my mind kept trailing with questions and playing events in my head. It focused on Lucien the most, on each look he gave me, his words… it all seemed like himself. Nothing suspicious, but he'd be stupid to give anything away. The frustration of everything was getting to me, and the temptation to stand and get myself a drink was so enormous my body was shaking. I tried to conceal this by wrapping the scarf around me so Ben wouldn't notice my growing agitation. I decided the fish and chips would do; I needed some grease. Ben stopped talking about the case and asked questions about my hobbies mostly. He watched movies when he had time, due to his demanding job.

'Just watching movies?' I asked.

'No, I do kickboxing. That I can do often.'

Music came on, and I recognised the dramatic intro of the violins right away. 'Woman' by Neneh Cherry. A song I hadn't heard in a long time. Ben stood to place the order, and he took out his wallet from the back of his jeans and put a few bills on the counter. He glanced at me, and I smiled at him. *I could make this work*, I thought. He was in my age group, which viewed the world different than the new generation, was good looking and sensible, and I felt safe around him. No drama, no mystery. He didn't feel like a puzzle I had to solve. He was simple and straightforward, but starting any romantic attachments was the last thing on my mind. I had to solve my issues before committing myself to someone.

Chapter Twenty-four

On Saturday, I was back in Greenwich for my lunch with Olivia. She told me to meet her near her house. I went there early and took a look at my old house that just stood there, taking up all that space. I had to call the real estate company to see where they were in the process of finding a new owner. I peered through Mrs. Parker's house, and it was hard to tell from where I stood, but it didn't look like she was at home. I crossed the street, but Olivia wasn't outside as she told me she would be. I stared at that yellow door as it stared back at me, and it seemed to get bigger and more imposing with each passing moment. My eyes went to Olivia's rose bush. I could ask her what she knew about the Black Baccara roses and catch her reaction. I glanced over my shoulder. The street was empty, and Mrs. Parker's curtains didn't move. She wasn't home, which was a relief. I wasn't in the mood to deal with her nonsense. She was nosy, and that was useful, but I didn't want to deal with her invitations for tea on this cloudy day.

I went to Olivia's driveway. There was a pathway that led to the back of the house, and the Mercedes wasn't there, so I nervously ran my hand over my hair and made my way to the back. There was a table and chairs, and there were bushes, but nothing resembled Black Baccara roses. Just to be certain, I did a Google search to see what the bushes looked like, but hers were different.

I pocketed the phone as I was about to turn and head to the front of the house. I paused, and my mouth went dry as my eyes went to the window. Olivia stood in the kitchen. She was in her coat and scarf, ready to leave. In front of her, leaning by the kitchen table, was Lucien. Her hands were across her chest, which suggested a defensive manner; Lucien had his hands placed firmly on the table, and his hair was pulled back into a ponytail with a ribbon. Olivia dropped her hands to the side and then threw them in the air. She put on leather gloves and grabbed her handbag as Lucien moved away from the table. If only I could be a fly on that wall to hear what they were talking about. They looked like they were in an argument. I moved away before they saw me, and I didn't want to imagine the look on their faces if they caught me. I hurried my steps to the front, and a text came in on my phone. It was Olivia, apologising for her tardiness and asking if I could meet her at the pub instead. What was so important that Lucien had to go to his old house? Didn't it affect him? All those memories of his mother in that kitchen that was always spotless with the smell of air freshener mixed with butter. Henry yelling or sitting by the TV, flipping the channels. I wondered what it smelled like now and what it looked like. Olivia had said she thought the house décor was something out of the eighties. And although she didn't say if she hired an interior designer, I imagined she would, and decorate it to her liking, bringing some life to the place. What was Lucien doing there? Was their relationship really just business? I hadn't replied to his text yet. It just sat there waiting. He had asked me to meet up with him again. I was still thinking about it, how he suddenly popped up and demanded I make time for him, as if he expected me to drop everything so he could grace me with his presence. I didn't want this to become a regular thing.

#

I ordered a Coke and found a table in one of the pub's window booths, and I saw Olivia looking impeccable in a red coat as she hurried to the pub. The door flung open seconds later, and she walked in. She whispered, 'I'm sorry,' as she turned her back to me to take a call. I took a sip of my Coke, watching her back, then she slipped her phone into her pocket and walked to the table.

'Emily,' she said, putting her arms around me as I stood to greet her. 'How are you?'

'I'm good, and you?' I asked.

'I'm good, very good. Business is going well, so I'm happy.'

Olivia didn't look like she was in an argument regarding her phone call – quite the contrary of that. She looked calm and relaxed.

'That's nice,' I said.

'So, what you have been up to?'

'Nothing much,' I lied, as the image of her with Lucien in her kitchen came back to me.

She started to tell me about her work and how well it was going, but I kept drifting off to what I saw.

'I wanted to ask if would you be interested in doing some marketing for my company?' she asked.

'Um… what are you looking for?' I asked.

'For someone to write content. The marketing company I hired is useless considering the fees I'm paying them. So, you can come to the company, and we will set a meeting there if you'd like?' she offered.

Me at her company? What if I ran into Lucien there? That would be awkward. However, they wouldn't do photo shoots in a boardroom but rather in a studio somewhere.

'Can I think about it?' I asked.

I was in no position to refuse work, but with all that had been going on, the roses and trying to understand the meaning behind it all, had taken so much time, I didn't know how I would be able to cope. So, after this lunch, I would work till late, sleep for a few hours, and go over to my parents' house for lunch the following day.

'Of course, I thought I would ask you first,' she said and reached for the menu.

As I took a sip of Coke, the bubbles danced in my mouth. 'I appreciate it.'

'You look lovely, by the way. Is there a man I need to know about?' she asked.

I thought of Ben, all serious and guarded. Then another thought came to me. She seemed quite interested if there was a man in my life. Why was that?

I opened the menu. 'No.'

I wanted to ask her about her life since hers seemed more interesting than mine, with Lucien and Jan parading around, but although I was dying to know, I couldn't ask about Jan. What could she possibly want with Jan? I thought of how she had put her arms around him the last time I had dinner with her. It looked like more than a professional relationship.

'I couldn't help but notice,' I said, changing the subject, 'the roses in your front yard.'

She looked up from the menu. 'Yes, it's a hobby of mine.'

'What do you know about Black Baccara roses?'

'Oh, now that is a lovely bunch of roses. They are a hybrid created in 2000. They are the symbol of love, well… all roses are. Why do you ask?'

'I'm working with a florist. I'm doing a bit of marketing for them, and I came across their name.'

This was a lie.

'Maybe I could buy the seeds and grow them, although winter is approaching. They hate cold weather,' she said.

'Do you know anyone who grows them?' I asked.

'No, not that I know of.'

We ordered our food, and the conversation drifted towards safe topics: how our week had been and plans for the weekend.

When we finished our meal, we parted ways outside the pub. I turned the corner and peered back at the road. I could still see her heading back towards her house. I needed to know more about this woman who had befriended me. I mean, let's face it, we hardly had anything in common.

I stayed behind as she walked briskly then stopped in front of the newsagent and waited. I entered the small convenience store just opposite and pretended to browse through the shelf by the window as I watched the road. Olivia stood with her hands across her chest as her hair moved softly with the breeze. I did a double take as Jan came from the other side, dressed in a red velvet blazer. Olivia dropped her hand to her side as he placed one hand on her waist and they gave each other pecks on the cheek before moving away.

I rushed out of the store and followed their route as I kept my eyes on them, but I stayed far enough behind so they wouldn't spot me. They walked casually, not holding hands or anything. Jan gestured with his hands as Olivia looked at him, charmed. She pointed at something, and Jan turned, causing my heart to roll into my ribcage as I dashed to a corner to avoid being seen. I took a peek from the corner and saw them get in a cab. A rush of desperation and curiosity rushed over me. I was at it again – following people around, looking for clues and answers. I hailed the upcoming taxi and told the driver to follow the other cab, and he cast me a dirty glance from the rear-view mirror. Olivia and Jan's cab was heading towards Canary Wharf. They stopped in front of a skyscraper and entered the tall building.

Chapter Twenty-five

I visited Anna at her father's house in Blackheath. It was raining so hard that I had difficulty navigating to the front door while holding the umbrella. Her father led me inside and rushed to hand me a towel, which was sweet of him. I shrugged out of my drenched coat and towel-dried my hair.

'It's raining cats and dogs out there,' he said. 'Tea?'

I nodded. 'Please.'

He gestured to the other room. 'Anna is in the living room.'

I smiled and walked towards the living room.

'Anna!' he shouted, which made me jump.

'I know, Dad, Emily is here. I heard her,' Anna shouted from the other end of the room.

'Do you want tea?' her father called out

'Yes, please!' she said.

Her black eye was still swollen, but it wasn't as black as before. A glass of water, a box of tissues and pain medication sat next to her on the table. The TV was on, and she was watching the Kardashians. I sat down across from her with my back to the TV. Anna rolled her eyes as if irritated by something and flipped the channel to watch something else, and thunder roared outside.

'I'm bored stiff,' she complained. 'All I do is sit by the TV all day, trying to find something suitable to watch.'

'Watch *Breaking Bad*!' her father yelled from the kitchen.

'He keeps urging me to watch that,' she said. 'It seems I'm the only person who hasn't watched it yet. Have you watched it?'

I crossed my legs. 'Yes.'

Anna looked at me curiously. 'Really? When?'

'With Ed,' I said.

'Oh,' she said, and we fell silent.

Another rumble of thunder rolled, and the rain slapped the windows. Mike came into the room holding two mismatched mugs of tea, and handed the red mug to Anna and the green to me.

'Anything else you ladies need?' he asked.

'We're good, Dad, thanks,' Anna said.

He smiled and walked out of the room.

Anna leaned forward. 'So, tell me something interesting. Please, please tell me you have been doing something. Anything.'

I took a sip of tea. Her father made a mean cup of tea. 'I met with Ben again.'

'Really? How did it go? What did you do? Tell me everything?' Anna said excitedly.

I told her all about my meeting with Ben, and she listened eagerly.

'Why didn't you tell me he came to question you?' I asked her after I finished.

She slapped her hand to her forehead. 'It completely slipped my mind. I thought it was nice of him to come by and ask me what had happened.'

'Lucien got in touch,' I blurted.

Anna spat out her mouthful of tea all over the coffee table. I blinked at her, shocked by this outburst, then I thought something was wrong.

'Are you okay in there?' Mike called out.

I reached for the box of tissues on the coffee table. 'We're fine!' I said.

'Oh no, he didn't,' Anna said.

I started to wipe the coffee table, avoiding eye contact. 'He did.'

'When? Where? How and why?'

I continued to clean the surface, and she leaned closer and whispered, 'Tell me you didn't sleep with him. Please tell me you didn't.'

I paused with my task and glanced at her. 'I didn't.'

'Whew, that's a relief. Why is he back?' Anna asked.

I curled the tissues into balls. 'He misses me.'

'How delightful now, after a year, but why are you speaking to him?'

'Because…' I paused. 'I was looking for him.'

There were so many weird things that had been happening to me that Anna knew nothing about. She had enough on her plate, and I didn't want to burden her with my problems.

'Why? Why can't you just let him go?' she asked.

I flumped down on the sofa, feeling exhausted by this conversation. 'I can't just do that. He has no one, and I told you the other day, it's about time he and I had a proper chat. Too much has happened.

'His mother could have killed you, and his father shouted hateful things at you,' Anna reminded me.

I reached for my mug of tea and cupped my hands around it. 'I can't blame him for his parents' actions. He is a good guy.'

Anna looked at me doubtfully. 'Is he?'

Was he? Was he the one responsible for all that happened so far? We sipped our tea as another rumble of thunder sounded in the distance.

'And you're seeing him regularly?' Anna asked.

I thought of the text that still sat there on my phone. 'No, he has a boyfriend.'

Anna raised an eyebrow. 'Really? Who?'

'You know him. It's Travis. Apparently, they got back together.'

'Oh, that scrawny little kid with pink hair. Ha!' she said. 'As if that would stop him.'

I looked at her questioningly. 'Stop him from what?'

'You know… trying to seduce you.'

I uncrossed my legs. 'He's not going to do that.'

She looked at me sharply. 'How do you know?'

'Because I won't let him.'

'You won't?'

'Have you met up with any of your exes?' I sighed.

'But he's not your ex, right? And yes, I have, and when I did, it all led to one place.'

'Where?' I asked.

She lowered her voice. 'In bed.'

'So, you're saying you can't be friends with an ex?' I asked.

'No,' she said.

'Are there any leads to your case?' I asked, changing the subject.

'No, nothing so far.' She paused, thinking of something, and took a sip of her tea.

'Do you girls need another cup of tea?' Mike called out.

'We're fine, Dad,' Anna called back.

I waited for her to go on.

Anna fingered the rim of the mug. 'I keep having this flashback.'

I peered at her. 'What sort of flashback?'

'It's distorted… chiffon,' she said.

I furrowed my eyebrows. 'Chiffon?'

'Yeah, I can't be sure… I think it's a sleeve of a shirt made of chiffon or lace.'

My blood went cold. Lucien and Jan liked to wear chiffon and lace shirts. Everything kept pointing at either of them, and there was the issue that the roses had stopped now that Lucien had reappeared in my life. I checked the app of the spy cam on my phone, but nothing suspicious came up so far.

'Did you tell the police about this?' I asked.

'No, not yet at least. I don't think it would be helpful.'

'Anything can be helpful.'

I thought of Olivia and Jan together getting inside that building. Were they having an affair? She was an attractive woman, but she was old enough to be his mum – not that that ever stopped anyone.

Chapter Twenty-six

He suggested a pub in Shoreditch, which was crowded with people on their night out. *What do we really do with our lives?* I thought. *We work and piss it off with booze to bury our issues, as I am doing with mine.* He was already there when I entered the pub. A glass of beer and a bottle of Coke sat on the table as Lucien peered up at me. He picked a spot in the corner that was dark, and I wondered if he was sneaking around so Travis wouldn't suspect anything. He was specific that it had to be on that particular day at that particular time, so I guessed that's when Travis would be out. I didn't want to be involved, but wasn't I already by agreeing to meet him? He looked more demure than usual, and his eyes were slightly bloodshot.

'Sorry for not replying to you earlier,' I said, sitting down.

'It's fine,' Lucien said. 'I know you have a lot on your plate, and I don't expect you to cancel everything for me.'

I detected a slight bitterness in his tone, and he looked moody. Perhaps there was a lover's tiff. Travis struck me as a demanding type, a bit of a diva, obnoxious and bitchy. I didn't know the lad and had only spoken to him once when he warned me to stay away from Lucien.

'I-I...' I stammered

His eyes climbed up to mine. 'Are you going to take off your coat?'

'Oh.' I stood and shrugged off my coat, placing it on the chair. He watched me carefully and then sipped his beer.

'Travis and I had a fight,' he announced.

No wonder he was in a mood. He cast me a sad glance and hid his eyes behind his long, thick lashes. I hoped this tiff wasn't about me or that he confronted Travis after what I told him when I made him promise not to say a word.

'You told him?' I asked.

He shook his head. 'No, this was about something else. Things haven't been good lately. Today I went to prison to visit my mum, and I was in no mood for his shit.'

The words 'prison' and 'mum' hung in the air. Why did he keep visiting her, knowing what she did? How could he even bring himself to look at her, let alone speak to her? He stood to get more beer, not offering anything to me. I checked the security app on my phone, but everything looked in order. I put the phone away as Lucien came back to the table, and he placed a glass of wine in front of me. I glanced up at him, and he was looking down at me, a smile forming on his lips as he took his seat across from me.

'What happened after… you know….'

He glared at me and ran his hand on the table. 'I told you my life fell apart.'

'But you didn't go into too much detail.'

'Is that what you want, details?'

'Yes….'

He broke eye contact. 'I was angry, and I was upset. I didn't know what to do or think. My mum, she….' He sighed and positioned himself upright. 'I got depressed and had to take time off from studying and work. I mean, my dad pushed my brother down in the well, and Mum came up with this crazy idea to cover it up and make it look like he was missing when he was dead.' His voice broke, and he took a sip of beer.

I took a sip of wine, not responding. What could I say? It was diabolical. They lied to Lucien, fooled people into thinking they were victims, and they got sympathy. Lucien had every right to know what had happened to his older brother.

Lucien lowered his head. 'They deceived me. They lied to me, but deep down, I knew. I always knew.'

'Knew?'

'We might have been half-brothers, but there was that bond. Each time I used to go to the house, I looked at that well, wondering how deep it was… little did I know….' He buried his head in his hands, visibly upset.

Amelia should consider herself lucky that her son kept visiting her in prison when he could have chosen not to have anything to do with her after what she had done to him. What she did to Sylvian, Amanda, and Ed. I was selfish. Compared to what Lucien had endured – how difficult what he went through had been – it was nothing compared to my struggles, yet I didn't see him drowning in bottles of wine and vodka. He held his head high and paddled on, and I had nothing but respect and admiration for him, to be that strong. To keep it together. Lucien removed his hands from his face, sniffed, took two more drinks of his beer, and placed the bottle down on the table.

'Do you think about him?' he asked.

'Who?'

'Your ex.'

'I do, yes,' I admitted. I leaned forward, and Lucien watched me with scepticism. 'I don't mean to overstep, and it's none of my business… but why do you go visit her after what she did?'

He took a large gulp of beer and placed the empty beer bottle on the table. 'She needs me. I'm the only one she has left.'

'But she killed….'

'It's hard to explain. Despite everything she did, killing those people and what she did to Sylvian…' He paused and sighed. 'I don't know… I guess I love her still.'

I leaned back in my chair and reached for my glass of wine.

'I wasn't getting many offers after what happened,' Lucien explained. 'Why would anyone want to work with a model whose parents were crazy? So, I shut off and stayed in bed most of the time. I had moved in with Jan at the time. He was supportive, and he helped.'

'Did you seek help?'

'Yeah, went to therapy. I didn't visit my mum right away. The therapist suggested I write her a letter first and express how I felt. It was the hardest letter I ever had to write.'

'What about Sasha?' I asked.

His eyes flickered at me. 'What about her?'

'Did she try to help you?'

'Yeah, but none of them could understand what I was going through. I spent the first six months working on myself, and the next six months getting my shit together and my life in order. I sold the house in Exeter, and then the one in Greenwich. Olivia helped me, too.'

Olivia helped him with what? Work? The image came to me again of them in her kitchen. Didn't she tell him we were friendly? Maybe she was giving it time. She couldn't mention my name without getting a reaction.

'What about photography? Do you still do that?' I asked.

'It's been put on hold for now. I can only focus on one thing at a time.'

'Such a pity.'

'What?'

'You are too talented to let it go,' I said,

'I didn't quit,' he said sharply. 'I'm just taking a break. I need to sort out the weird stuff that has been going on.'

The hairs on the back of my neck stood on end. 'What weird stuff?'

He glanced at the door, and I did the same. Was someone out there? He reached for his phone that was lying face down on the table while I waited, panicking deep down.

'I got these,' he said, sliding his phone towards me.

It was like the sky had fallen onto my head as I glanced at the image; it lay on a doormat like mine was. A Black Baccara rose.

Chapter Twenty-seven

I felt the colour drain from my face. Lucien slid the screen and another photo appeared. Another rose on the doormat, this time with a message. Black spots appeared in my vision, so I shut my eyes as he flicked the screen again to get a close-up of the message.

Burning for a love that feels like war
With ravenous desire, the eyes with their wicked shine
to take a glimpse of the eternally beautiful.

My tongue grew fat, making me unable to speak. I reached for the glass of wine and drained it. Lucien watched me with curiosity.

'What?' he asked.

I couldn't bear it. Both of us were getting these flowers, but unlike mine, his message read like a love note. I had to eliminate him from my list of suspects. He wouldn't send flowers and write a message to himself. That would be insane. I grabbed my coat and walked out without saying a word. I heard him call after me, but I didn't want to be there a minute longer. I needed to be alone to think. I breathed in the cold air as a black cab drove by.

I hailed for it and got in just in time so Lucien wouldn't try to stop me and bombard me with questions. There was a pattern going on here, but what did it all mean? We were being targeted by the same person. Why? Who was doing this? My phone went off, but I ignored it.

#

The phone calls and the texts didn't stop, but I ignored them while driving myself to work. Olivia sent me an email to meet up, and I ignored that too. I wanted to get my head around what was happening. The two of us got the same exact roses with a message. Mine read like a threat; his were more of a declaration of love. I should have asked him when he got those roses to see if the dates aligned with each other, and where else he got them. In the block of flats where Jan lived? Did this someone go inside and drop the rose on the doormat? Were there cameras in that complex? Did he inform the police? Should I tell Ben? No, probably that wouldn't be a good idea for many reasons. I couldn't go behind Lucien's back, and there was the issue of Lucien and me. Ben and I had just met up twice, and it was still casual between us. It wasn't like we were dating or anything. What was I doing with Ben? I liked him, but what was I to him? Someone who had issues, no doubt, where he might have felt a little sorry for me. I lay in bed, listening to the rain trickling softly against the windows and the tires of cars whooshing on the wet roads. There were odd voices from random people or neighbours passing by outside, and a dog was barking – sounds of everyday life – while I hid away from it.

I had a dream that I was standing on a cliff. I was not sure where, but it was a cloudy day, and the wind lashed my body as the cold swept into my bones. Instead of water, there were rose petals, a sea of them so dark red they looked almost black, and someone gave me a hard shove, making me tumble down to the petals. My eyes sprung open, and I sat up straight. I rubbed my face with my hands and lay my head back on the damp pillow. It was dark out, and I had no idea what time it was. My hand fiddled on the bedside table, looking for my phone. It dropped on the floor, and I stretched to pick it up. Luckily the screen didn't break. Ten o'clock. I groaned into the darkness; the only light came from outside. I got up from the bed, turned on the lights, made my way to the kitchen and put the kettle on.

While I waited, I checked the security app on my phone. The camera looked directly at the front door. I fast forwarded it, but apart from me going out to take the rubbish and the postman delivering the mail, nothing was out of the ordinary. I made myself a strong cup of coffee and, yawning, went to my desk where my laptop lay open on a copywriting piece I was working on. I thought of Olivia's offer to do marketing for her company. Would it be a good idea to mix business with pleasure? I could be professional, and I'd be working from home. There was no need for me to work at the office apart from the occasional meeting. Maybe I could set up an appointment with her and see what she had in mind and how much she was willing to offer. As I was about to sit, there was pounding on the door and then the shriek of the doorbell.

'Emily!'

I shut my eyes. Why couldn't he just leave me alone? Didn't he take the hint I didn't want to talk to him?

'I know you're in there. Your lights are on,' Lucien announced

'For Christ's sake,' I muttered under my breath as I rushed to the door as the doorbell screamed again.

'What?' I hissed. 'Why can't you leave me alone?'

Lucien sized me up. 'Why are you not answering my calls?'

'Because I don't want to talk to you,' I protested.

'Why?' he demanded. 'What have I done?'

'You've done nothing.'

He sighed and nipped inside, shutting the door behind him, and I turned away from him.

'What the fuck, Emily?' he shouted.

Lucien was a calm person who hardly raised his voice or lost his temper, but he had a before and after, like me. The Lucien of now wasn't as collected. We had become more alike than we liked to admit. I crossed my hands across my chest and looked at the floor. I was in thick, fleece socks, and one of them had a hole in the toe that I didn't notice before. I dragged my feet to the chair and slumped down. I was exhausted, feeling grumpy and miserable, even though I had taken a long nap. Lucien eyeballed me, waiting for an explanation.

'Well?' he said impatiently.

'I got them too,' I said in a low voice.

'Got what?'

'The roses, and one of them had a message.'

He paced around the living room, eyeing me. 'You got roses, too?' He looked around the house. 'Where are they?'

'In an evidence bag.'

He rose his eyebrows. 'You told the police about it?'

I ran my hand on the laptop. 'Yes, I gave them to Ben. He's looking into it.'

Lucien raised an eyebrow in surprise. 'Ben? As in DC Miller?'

'Yes. The detective who was investigating Ed's disappearance and your case—'

'I know who he is,' he snapped. 'And what? You remained in touch with him?'

'No, I ran into him, and we met for a drink and—'

'I see,' he said.

That 'I see' spoke a thousand words. I stared at Lucien, him staring into space, working it all out and jumping to the wrong conclusions. I didn't have to explain anything to him. *Let him think what he wants*, I thought. He shagged whomever he liked, but I couldn't help wondering if he was jealous. Why should he be? To evoke jealousy, there had to be desire involved.

Chapter Twenty-eight

'Did you go to the police with the roses?' I asked.

'No, anyone could have sent them. I have a fan base. It could be someone who is obsessed, hence why I disabled my social media accounts,' Lucien explained.

'You were harassed?' I asked.

'Strangers were asking me all sort of questions. It started to get to me.'

'So, you think it is one of your stalkers doing this? Why send me the flowers, then?'

'That's what I would like to know.'

I took a sip of my now-cooling coffee.

'Can I have a coffee?' Lucien asked. 'Actually, I'll help myself.'

He disappeared into my small kitchen, and I heard the switch of the kettle. I stood and found him with his hands on his hips, scrutinising my kitchen. The mugs and plates on the drying rack and the single bottle of wine by the bin. He took a mug that said s*assy* on it, picked up a teaspoon from the drying rack, and helped himself to my jar of coffee that stood on the counter.

'I think you should go to the police,' I suggested. 'They would take it more seriously if there were two of us.'

'Go to your boyfriend, you mean?' he asked. 'Why didn't you tell me you were dating the copper?'

I rolled my eyes. 'I'm not dating him. We're friends.'

'Of course, you are,' he said.

He made no effort to hide the bitterness in his tone.

'Because *we're* friends, aren't we, Emily?' he asked.

'Why are you being like this?'

'Like what?'

'Immature and childish.'

He leaned against the doorway, gazing down at me. 'Childish?'

I studied his face. 'You have a boyfriend, and the real issue is the flowers, not who is sleeping with whom.'

'I don't like to label things. I thought you knew that,' he remarked while stirring his coffee.

I rubbed my forehead with my hands. 'Whatever, Lucien. Someone is out there fucking with my head,' I said.

'How many flowers did you get?' he asked.

'Two here, the other at… my old house.'

He looked at me, shocked by this. 'Someone went into your old house?'

'Yes.'

'And who has keys to your house?'

'Me and the realtor.'

'When did you go to your house?'

'A few weeks ago, to speak to Mrs. Parker.'

'Ah, good old Agnes,' he said.

I looked him up and down as he leaned against the counter, his hands cupping the mug.

'I met Olivia,' I said.

I waited for a reaction, but his face remained neutral. 'Yeah, she told me. She thought you were crazy at first, pounding on her door. She didn't say what it was about. We don't talk about that.'

'What do you talk about?'

'I'm working for her, and we have better things to discuss,' he said, walking past me.

I followed him out of the kitchen. He sat down on the sofa and propped his feet up on the coffee table. I was unsure how to feel about how he was making himself at home. There he was invading my house, my personal space.

'What did your message say?' he asked. 'Did you take a photo of it?'

'I don't document each detail of my life.'

'Do you remember, at least?' he asked.

'It wasn't as poetic as yours, and mine was shorter, something about how rose petals and bloodstains lie on my path.'

'Bloodstains?'

'Yes. I don't want to think about it,' I said, sitting on the armchair.

I lifted the mug to my lips, but the coffee had gone cold. I stood and went back to the kitchen to make a fresh one. Lucien was checking his phone when I re-emerged into the living room. Was it Travis demanding where he was?

'What did the copper tell you about the roses?' he asked, pocketing his phone.

I placed the coffee mug on the desk. 'He said the roses weren't bought from a florist but grown from a garden at home. They are called the Black Baccara, a hybrid type of rose. Do you know anyone who grows these types of roses?'

'No,' Lucien said. 'What about the card?'

'What about it?' I asked.

'Were there any prints?'

I sat down on the armchair. 'No.'

'So, it's a dead-end.'

'He's still looking into it. Anna got attacked.'

His eyes went wide. 'Anna got attacked? When?'

'A few weeks ago.'

'A few weeks ago? And you're just telling me now? What else are you keeping from me?'

'I'm not keeping it from you. I just… I don't know, but I think it's all related – the roses, the messages, Anna being attacked.'

'How was she attacked?' he asked.

After I finished telling him, he asked, 'When was this? Do you remember the day?'

I thought about this. 'It was a Friday.'

'Do you remember the date?'

Why was it so important?

'Um… let's see,' I said, reaching for the calendar on my desk. I ran my finger on the Fridays and paused at the twenty-fifth and told him the date. Lucien looked away, contemplating. Did he know something?

I stood from the chair. 'What's wrong?'

He stood. 'Nothing, but I have to go.'

'Go where?' I protested.

'Home.'

Lucien placed his hand on my arm and rubbed it gently. 'Just sit tight.' He gave me a peck on the cheek, and I stood there confused as he showed himself out.

Chapter Twenty-nine

I walked past the businessmen and women in their black coats and brief cases, talking or typing on their phones. The air was crisp and the sky was blue with a few clouds looming over in Canary Wharf, where Olivia's office was.

I entered the building where people in suits marched through the reception area, all knowing where they were going. I walked towards the marbled front desk and told the man dressed in a sharp suit who I was. He made me walk under a metal detector and ran my bag under the scanner after he took my information. I felt like I was going in the House of Commons, not for a meeting with the director of a cosmetic company. After the security checks had been made, I was given a card that read VISITOR and was told that Olivia's office was located on the thirtieth floor. I adjusted my suit as the lift slowly went up and stopped at the fifteenth floor, where I was engulfed by suits, a few talking about profit margins and others about bitcoin. No one noticed I was there, but why should they?

I breathed in the mix of perfumes, cologne, and sweat as the lift closed and carried on. The lift stopped at the twentieth floor, where the suits got out, and I was alone once again. The lift pinged, and I was faced with a glassed door and another marbled reception area. I pushed the door open as 'Atomic' by Blondie played, which didn't quite go with the modern décor and the bare white walls with pictures of models with radiant skin. A girl with brown skin stood behind the desk and smiled pleasantly at me as I told her who I was, and she gestured at the love seat for me to sit. So, Olivia was a woman with expensive taste who had good taste in music. I wondered what sort of modelling Lucien was going to do for her, since he was an alternative model who didn't quite fit with her brand. Neither Olivia nor Lucien were specific on what he was going to do. Olivia appeared, dressed in a black designer suit, her white-blonde hair cascading below her shoulders. I couldn't get over how much she looked like Amelia when she was younger. They both had the same big, almond-shaped green eyes and delicate bone structure. She stretched out her arms to me as I stood, and we gave each other pecks on the cheeks, then my phone went off, the sound loud and piercing.

'I'm sorry,' I said.

'Not to worry.'

I fumbled in my bag and scowled at the screen. What did Lucien want? I stared at the phone in my hand, as if it were a bomb.

'Are you going to get that? It could be important.' Olivia pointed out.

'No, it's fine,' I replied, rejecting the call and turning the phone to vibrate.

I followed Olivia through a narrow corridor. I expected offices with desks and chairs, printers jamming and hassled staff, but there were just rooms with closed grey doors. She opened another glassed door, where I made out an oval oak table. Olivia held the door open for me as I nipped inside. The room had a view of the skyscrapers and the Thames spreading across. There was a grey fitted carpet and more pictures of perfect-looking women hanging on the walls. Olivia gestured for me to sit on one of the executive chairs.

'Can I get you anything?' she offered.

'A glass of water, please,' I said.

She picked up the phone on the desk and ordered tea and water.

'Blondie,' I said.

'Excuse me?' she said.

'Um… The band… Debbie Harry,' I said.

'Oh yes, I loved her as a young girl. My mum used to listen to her songs. You don't hear music like this any more,' she said flipping her hair and sitting on the chair across from me. 'So, how are you?'

'I'm good,' I said.

A man dressed in a black shirt and smart, black trousers walked in carrying a tray with a pot of tea and a glass of water.

'So,' she said after he walked out. 'The job is simple really. I need someone to write content for our website and write a good brief of our products when we advertise them. You are familiar with Facebook ads, I assume?'

'Yes.'

'Are you familiar with my brand? Tried any of the products?'

'No, I mean… I am familiar with the brand, but I haven't tried any of the products.'

I researched her company for hours before coming here, to be prepared.

She smiled. 'I'll give you a few samples for you to try on. Your skin looks tired, and there are bags under your eyes.'

'Oh,' I said.

She never told me that before, out of politeness perhaps, but with all that had been going on, skin care was the least of my worries. I had applied concealer this morning to hide the bags under my eyes, but a woman who did cosmetics for a living could tell that I needed a new brand of concealer.

'Are you getting enough sleep?' she asked.

I thought this meeting was about her company, not about how bad my skin looked.

'Not really,' I admitted.

She stood and went to a basket that I hadn't noticed before, sitting up on a cabinet, and chose a few samples.

'Dry skin?' she asked.

'Yep,' I said.

She came to the desk and set down white packets with silver designs on the desktop.

'This is to take care of the uneven skin tone, this for dullness, and this is an eye cream to help with the dark circles. Apply some cucumber to soothe the puffiness and drink lots of water,' she advised.

'Right,' I said.

I felt the phone buzz in my bag on my lap. Olivia seemed to hear it too, but said nothing.

'So that's all you need from me?' I asked, to drown out the buzzing in my bag.

'I want you to look at the analytics, compare the figures every month, and give me the demographics of who's going on the website. We are more online-based nowadays, as the internet rules the world.'

'Right,' I said.

She reached for the notepad beside the phone and scribbled something on it, then slid the pad to me. I peered at it. The figure was double the amount I charge. It was too much, but I needed the money.

'Would that work?' she asked.

'You don't have to—'

'Please, Emily, I'm not going to negotiate a fee with you. Take it. I'm sure you are more than capable. You don't have any idea the relief you have given me. I know I can trust you.'

'Thank you,' I said. 'Will I work from home, or do I need to come here?'

'From home, and you will give me updates by email. Then, we can meet over coffee or dinner like we were doing. Do you mix business with pleasure, Emily?'

I was thrown by the question.

Buzz, buzz.

I shut my eyes. *I'm going to kill him,* I thought. Did he think the world revolved around him? What was it that it couldn't wait? Olivia stood, dismissing me, and told me she had another meeting in fifteen minutes. I stood as Olivia opened the door for me. I thanked her, and she told me she would email me to meet for dinner. The phone was still buzzing in my bag, and I clutched my hands into fists with irritation. I shoved my hand inside my bag to find my phone. A man appeared at the end of the corridor, beautifully dressed and adorned in jewellery. This was her other meeting? I gaped at Jan as he walked past me.

'Emily darling,' he said, casting me the most dazzling smile.

I watched as the buzzing from my phone went on insistently, demanding my attention. Jan swaggered to the corridor where Olivia held the door open for him. He walked inside and she looked at him as if he were the most precious thing before she closed the door.

#

'*What?*' I hissed at the phone when I left the building. 'Why do you keep calling me?'

'Something happened,' Lucien said.

'What? You got another rose?' I asked as I walked past the businessmen and tourists. 'If that's the case, call the police!'

'No, it's Sasha.'

I stopped dead in my tracks as a chill went through me. 'What happened?'

'She has been attacked.'

Chapter Thirty

Still shaken by what Lucien told me, I went home. A pile of mail was waiting for me, so I collected it off the floor and took it with me to the kitchen. I rested my hand on the counter, staring down at the mail. First Anna, and now Sasha had been attacked. This news left me perturbed and afraid. Was I next? I thought of Jan swaggering past me in the corridor. Was it him doing this? Would he attack his own friend? When was Sasha attacked? And where? Lucien didn't get into much detail. It seemed Jan hadn't been informed yet. Would he still go to the meeting if he knew? That was cold. I guessed he had no idea. My phone buzzed, and I reached for it. It was a text from Lucien warning me to stay home and not go out at night alone. Not that I would, and I didn't have much of a social life anyway. I opened the fridge, poured myself a glass of wine to soothe my nerves and went to the sofa to text him back.

When was Sasha attacked, and where?

A reply came right away.

I'll come by. It will be late, though.

I called my parents, then I had a long bath with a glass of wine for company and shut my eyes to rest them for a bit.

The well stood in the living room of my old house. Red water flew and bodies were spit out: Amanda's, Ed's, and Sylvian's. My eyes snapped open and I placed my hand over my head. Why I was having dreams about that well? What did it mean? A heavy pounding came from the front door, making me jump out of my skin, and I accidentally splashed water onto the floor. I reached for my phone and checked the security app. It was Lucien. I put on my robe as I stepped out of the bath. I nearly slipped on the puddle of water, so I held onto a towel rail for dear life while my heart jolted into my ears. The pounding came again, softer now.

'The door is open!' I shouted.

I heard the door open, then close, and the lock turn. I got into my tatty sweater and sweatpants as a funny pain grew in my ankle. I opened the bathroom door and Lucien was in the living room. I hopped to the sofa to sit next to him, and he stood abruptly.

'What happened?' he asked.

'I nearly slipped in the… bath. I think I twisted my ankle,' I said, sinking down on the sofa.

He went into the kitchen without saying anything, and I heard him open the freezer and take out something. He re-emerged holding a packet of peas, the same as he had a year ago. He knelt in front of me and gently placed it on my ankle.

He held my foot with his hand. 'Don't call out like that, that you're in the house.'

I gazed down at him. 'I knew it was you.'

He looked up. 'How?'

'I have a spy cam just above the door.'

'Oh,' he said.

'How's Sasha?'

'In shock and in pain.'

'Do you know how it happened?'

'She was attacked while out with friends from hers from work. Her face is black and blue. Her nose is broken; so are a few of her ribs.'

Another woman attacked while out with friends. There was a cycle going on here.

'Was she… drinking?' I asked.

'She had a few drinks, yes, but she wasn't plastered.'

'Was she alone?'

'She left the pub to meet with Lloyd. She was going to the tube, and that was when it happened.'

'In the tube?'

'No, nearby the tube. Someone came from behind her and…'

'It's the same thing that happened to Anna. The assailant came from behind her while she was going to pick up her bag,' I explained.

'The police are looking into it too, but I doubt they catch who did it.'

'Aren't there any security cameras?'

'I don't know.'

My foot was still in his possession with the packet of peas firmly placed on my ankle, so I was unable to move away from him. Instead, I stared down at Lucien, and I noticed the lilac dye was fading off and his blonde hair was more visible.

'Did you have a disagreement with someone?' I asked.

He looked up. 'What do you mean?'

'Did you have a row with someone who is doing this?'

'No,' he said. 'I don't go around arguing with people. I'm not a hothead, you know that.'

He was offended by this. I knew that. *But do we really know the people around us? Everyone has their secrets, or a side of them that they are ashamed to reveal*, I thought.

'Does Sasha recall anything?' I asked.

He shook his head. 'No.'

It made me feel like shit that I thought, somehow, she had been involved when she fell victim to this. This type of attack wasn't typical of a woman.

'Does Jan know Sasha is in the hospital?'

'Yes, he came to visit when I was about to leave. Why?'

'I saw him at Olivia's office,' I said.

He peered at me with scepticism. 'And what were you doing at Olivia's office?'

'She offered me a job,' I said.

He crooked an eyebrow. 'Did she now?'

'Yes, she needs someone to help her with marketing.'

'It makes sense she would ask you. I had no idea you two were that close. She didn't make it sound like you were,' he said.

'We're friendly,' I said. 'What are you going to do for her?'

'What do you mean what am I going to do for her? She needs a male model, and I'm a model, so… she might need me to take a few photographs for her models as well.'

'What is Jan doing for her?'

His eyes bore into me. 'What is this?'

'All the times I have met up with Olivia, Jan always seemed to be there,' I explained.

Lucien stood and paced around the room, still holding the packet of peas. 'You're doing it again, aren't you?'

'Doing what?'

'Going around asking questions.'

'I'm just curious, I mean… he's… well… gorgeous….'

'Yes,' Lucien agreed. 'He is, isn't he?'

'I just said that he is.'

He gave me a look that I couldn't quite place.

He came closer and handed me the packet of peas. His face was only inches away from mine, and I could feel his breath on my skin. 'Do you want him, Emily?'

I made a disgusted face. '*What*? No!'

Lucien smiled. 'Why not? You just admitted to finding him attractive.'

'He is attractive, but it doesn't mean I want to jump into bed with him.'

'Because you'd rather have the policeman,' he remarked.

I glared at him as tiny sparks of anger ignited in me. 'What is this? Why are you asking me this? Since when did you become insecure?'

'I should go,' he announced.

I made an attempt to stand, but I flinched in pain.

'I'll show myself out. Make sure you lock the door,' he warned.

Chapter Thirty-one

Anna, wearing a baseball cap and sunglasses to hide her injuries, came to see me the next day. I peered over her shoulder to where her dad was parked out front, and he waved at me. I waved back and ushered Anna in. She looked around the place and then settled on the sofa.

'Open a window, Emily. This place stinks,' she complained.

'Can I get you anything?' I asked, ignoring her statement.

She removed the baseball cap, and her blonde hair fell into waves over her shoulders. It needed a trim and a wash, but her bruises had almost healed. Her nose was still bandaged, though, and the scar above her eyebrow was still visible.

'Coffee would be great,' she said.

I nodded, limped into the kitchen to put the kettle on, and noticed the peas were still on the counter. *Since when did I become this messy?* It had defrosted completely, so I decided it would be a good idea to make pea soup with it. With my dinner sorted for that evening, I opened the fridge, placed the peas there, and took out the milk.

'How are you?' I asked after I handed Anna a mug of coffee.

'I've seen better days. I heard there was another attack, and that it was Sasha this time.'

'Who told you?'

'The detective came to ask me more questions and mentioned that another girl got attacked. He refused to tell me who at first, but then he told me.'

'Which detective?' I asked.

'Your detective.'

'He is not *my* detective.'

She took a sip of coffee. 'It's probably the same person who attacked me.'

'I think so too,' I said.

'Wait,' she said. 'How did you know Sasha got attacked? Did Ben tell you?'

'No, Lucien did.'

'Of course, I forgot you are back with him,' she said.

'I am not *back* with him. We're friends.'

'Yeah, as if anyone could remain friends very long with *that*,' she said, exasperated.

'Anna,' I said, 'I'm exhausted. I have no energy to argue about this. I know you disapprove, so we'll just leave it at that. Did you tell Ben what you told me about the chiffon shirt?'

'Yes, I told him.'

'And what did he say?'

'Nothing, just that he would look into it. It's all he says. He doesn't tell me anything.'

Did Ben suspect that it was linked just like I did, and was running his own little investigation? I had to call him and suggest a drink to find out what he was up to.

'It takes time to catch who it is,' I said.

'Yeah, well….' She sighed. 'I just don't understand why you're so obsessed with that guy.'

I blinked at her. 'We have been through this, Anna. I'm not obsessed.'

'What if, somehow, he has something to do with all of this?'

'He doesn't,' I said

Her eyebrows furrowed. 'How do you know?'

'Because….' I stopped myself.

Anna waited for me to elaborate. I stood and limped a little as I ran my hand through my hair. Anna looked down at my socked feet, noticing for the first time since she arrived that I was hobbling.

'Why are you limping? Are you hurt, too?' she asked, genuinely concerned.

'I just twisted my ankle while getting out of the bath,' I said. 'I'll be fine.'

'You should be careful, but you were saying?' she prompted.

'Sasha is his friend. Lucien wouldn't attack his own friend, would he?'

'I don't know. Wasn't he, like, sleeping with her? Maybe they had a quarrel and—'

'He's not like that,' I said.

'His mother killed people, and his father pushed his brother down a well. His parents are messed-up people. He can be just as messed up if not worse, and you don't know what experience he might have.'

'It can't be him,' I snapped. 'Because he is going through the same thing as I am.'

Anna's face was a mask of concern. 'What do you mean going through the same thing as you? What is going on?'

Without thinking, I blurted out some of what I had been keeping from Anna.

'Emily, please tell me all of it,' she demanded.

I hopped back on the sofa, and I told her about the roses. Her eyes grew wider and wider as all that had been going on took shape in her head.

'And you didn't think to tell me about any of this?'

'I didn't want to worry you,' I said.

'Worry me? I was attacked. Do you have any idea how scary that is? How frightened I felt? And you didn't want to worry me? This might be the same person… if you had said something, I wouldn't….'

She stood abruptly.

'Anna—'

She raised her hand as if to keep me quiet.

'I'm going to go now. I have to be on my own to process this.'

'But—'

'Shut up, Emily, stop talking,' she said, charging to the front door and slamming the door behind her.

I stared at the front door as I heard the humming of an engine outside, then a car door being slammed and a car driving away. *Great* I thought. *My friend blames me for what has happened, and now she hates me.*

I sat on the sofa for what felt like hours, even if it was just a few minutes. I exhaled deeply and stood, then limped to the bathroom. I opened the medicine chest and dry swallowed two pain killers. I turned and glanced down at the bath, which needed to be cleaned. I was going to reach for a sponge, and I blinked at the floor. Something was shimmering in the same spot where I almost slipped. I scrutinised it to see if it was water, but it would have dried out by now. I knelt down using the bath to balance myself and stared at the shiny bit, then I ran my hand over it and the texture felt like… grease.

Chapter Thirty-two

My shoulders went tight as I squirmed away from the bathroom. Had someone been in my house? How? But I would have seen it with the camera. I checked the app twice a day, and there was no unusual activity. I was sure I didn't use grease in the bathroom. I limped to the kitchen and opened the cupboard where the hardware and detergents were and inspected the bottles one by one. Washing liquid, fabric conditioner, floor detergents, window cleaner, bleach and grease. It seemed silly to obsess over something like this, but it was suspicious. Anna had been in the house just now, but she didn't use the bathroom.

Lucien had been coming here regularly, but his visits were brief, and he never used the bathroom either. And I would have seen him carrying the bottle. Then what was it? I could call Ben and tell him… what? There was a small splash of grease, and I nearly slipped on my back? The fall could have been fatal. I limped to the living room. I could see the bathroom from where I stood, and dread curled into my stomach. I rechecked the security footage going back to when I had it installed. There was me going in and out, the postman, Lucien, and Anna's visit, but nothing else. I glanced over my shoulder as a breath caught in my throat. There was the back door that I never used and didn't think to install a camera over. *Stupid, stupid, stupid*. I stood and tottered to the back door that was located in the kitchen. I turned the knob with my heart in my throat, the fear gripping my insides like an iron fist. It was locked. Did someone come in from the window? I had no security inside the house, but I always made sure all the windows were locked when I left. I sat on the kitchen chair, staring into space, hideously afraid more now than ever.

#

I sat on the sofa with my knee jittering. A glass of vodka sat on the table, and I jumped at every sound. I couldn't take it. I wanted it over and done with, so I could get on with my life. I should be writing the piece for Olivia, but there I sat, unable to focus or do anything. I had to deliver what I had promised, or she would fire me. I tried to call Anna, but my call was diverted to voicemail. I put music on to block the silence and limped towards the windows from time to time. It was dark out, the streets were empty and most of the other houses' lights were on. I saw him coming towards the house, and I shuffled to the door and opened it as he was about to knock.

'Still hurts?' Lucien asked and walked past me.

I shut and bolted the door after him. 'I will be fine. How is Sasha?'

'In pain.' He gazed down at the floor. 'If I find out who did this, I'll kill him.'

'Now, there will be no killing of anyone. You should know better.'

'You should rest,' he said, and he helped me to the sofa. 'Have you eaten?'

I shook my head. 'I'm not hungry.'

'You look anxious. What's wrong?'

'I think someone was here.'

Lucien's eyebrows furrowed. 'Here at this house?'

'Yes, but I'm not sure… I found grease in the bathroom. That's why I twisted my ankle.'

His face turned serious. 'Did you call the police?'

I shook my head. 'As I said, I could be wrong.'

He stood, plodded towards the bathroom and inspected the floor. He crouched down, took out his phone and snapped a picture of the floor. He pocketed the phone, then he ran his hand on the shimmering bit, felt the texture between his fingers and smelt it. Our eyes met from across the room. He stood and returned back to the living room.

'I'm going to get you out of here,' he said.

'What? No!'

'You come and stay with us.'

'Us?'

'Jan and me.'

It should be the least of my concerns, but what happened to Travis? Wasn't Travis living with them?

'Oh no, I can't.'

'You're not safe here.'

'I appreciate this, but I'm not going—'

'It's either Jan or Olivia.'

Olivia? Where did she fit in all of this?

Lucien slid next to me, reading the confusion on my face. 'I wasn't completely honest with you.'

I squirmed away from him. *No more surprises. I won't be able to handle it.* Lucien's posture stiffened.

I managed to gather enough saliva to speak. 'About what?'

'Olivia, she's….' His words vanished.

'She's? What? Your lover?'

His eyes went wide. '*No!* That would be disgusting.'

'Why would it be disgusting?'

'Because we are related.'

My mouth gaped open. 'You and Olivia are related? How?'

I didn't know why I sounded surprised, but I was. The icy looks, the white-blonde hair and the delicate, striking facial features were a dead giveaway. My mind went back to the past events as if on rewind. Her interest in me, Lucien being in the house, and now her friendship with Jan made sense. She befriended me to see what made me… what? Appealing to Lucien? Why me? What made me special? I was no one special, just an ordinary woman who went through fucked-up situations.

'Yes, she's my mum's first cousin.'

'But—but—'

'I didn't tell you because… well… nobody knows apart from Jan and Sasha,' he explained.

'But she bought your house?' I asked.

He looked down at his hands. 'Yes, she bought it off me. Of course, I tried to refuse, but she wanted to give me the money… She helped me a lot. After what had happened… she came and looked after me. She helped me get back on my feet.'

My skin prickled as I buried my face with my hands. 'Why didn't she tell me any of this?'

'Because I told her not to, and it was best to be kept… quiet with all that had happened.'

'You mean hidden?'

He turned to me. 'In a way. Look, this might sound shocking to you, but it was for the best. Olivia and my mum weren't close. Mum wouldn't even let me visit her, but I used to go without her knowledge to see Olivia. Olivia had a house in Notting Hill before she moved to Greenwich. I'm telling you because I trust you, and I would appreciate it if you keep it between us.'

'So, what she said….'

'The truth,' he assured me.

'And she befriended me because….'

'Because she likes you, nothing else. She's a good woman. Now I can take you to the house—'

I tried to stand, but I winched in pain and flumped back on the sofa.

'There is no way I'm going back there!' I argued.

'Jan it is, then.'

'No! I will not let you carry me about like I'm a parcel,' I protested. 'I'm still processing all of this.'

'What is the issue anyway?'

'So basically, I'm working for—'

'I work for her, too. What difference does it make? Money is money. It doesn't matter where it comes from.'

'Where does Jan fit in all of this?'

'Jan is helping her with a few things. He used to come with me when I would visit her. That is why she's so fond of him. They are not having an affair, if that's where you're getting at.'

'I didn't say that,' I said.

'But you sure as hell has thought it.' He stood. 'You're always jumping to the wrong conclusions, Emily.'

'I assumed you were related,' I said. 'The icy looks gave you away.'

He turned, smiling down at me. 'Icy?'

'You know what I mean.' I sighed. 'I'm tired. I'm going to bed.'

'You're not staying here,' he argued.

'Lucien, please… I'm not going to stay with you, your friend, and your boyfriend.'

'Boyfriend?' he asked.

'Yeah, Travis, remember him?'

He stood like a statue in my living room, gazing lazily at me.

'He's not my boyfriend any more.'

I shook my head. 'I can't deal with this right now.'

'You don't have to deal with anything. First, he was my "boyfriend," but now he's not.' He made air quotes on *boyfriend*.

'And why is that? If you don't mind me asking?'

'It wasn't working out, and we want different things.'

'And what would that be?'

Right then, it came to me why he might have broken the relationship off. Lucien kept staring at me.

'Oh no, no, no,' I said. 'It happened once. It won't happen again.'

'What?' he asked, smiling. 'You think me breaking up with Travis has something to do with you? You're a beautiful woman, but you think highly of yourself.'

'Excuse me?'

'Besides,' he said, ignoring my statement, 'you are with the copper, right? You want me to help you get to bed?'

'No, I'll manage.'

'Fine, I'll stay and sleep on the sofa.'

'Go home, Lucien, to your bed. I'll be fine.'

'I don't have a home. My home has been gone since Sylvian was gone.'

He lowered his head, and his sadness engulfed the room. He had everything, yet he lost it all. His parents had hidden a secret for so long that their deception wasn't something to be forgotten or forgiven. I felt sorry for this beautiful young man, and I couldn't say no, so I let him sleep on the sofa. It was the least I could do, to let him mourn for what his life would have been if his half-brother was still alive.

Chapter Thirty-three

My sleep was restless, and at six o'clock in the morning, I gave up and left the bedroom. Lucien was lying on the sofa, asleep. Thanks to the pain medication, my ankle felt better, and I could walk like a normal person. I tip-toed towards the sofa and looked down at this miraculous bloke, his chest rising and falling as he slept peacefully, and I felt a pinch of envy. How could he sleep with all that had been happening? I lifted the throw over him and turned away, trying not to make a noise. I put the kettle on and stared at the window, watching the sun rising. Outside, the streets were quiet. Most of the neighbours were safely in their beds where no harm would come to them. I sat on the chair in the kitchen, drinking my coffee, as I heard soft rustling coming from the living room. Lucien appeared by the doorway a few moments later, rubbing his eyes.

'Good morning,' I said.

'Morning, what are you doing up so early?'

'Couldn't sleep. Did I wake you?'

'The kettle did.'

I stood.

'No,' he said. 'I'll do it. How is your ankle?'

'Better.'

We fell quiet while Lucien made the coffee then sat across from me at the table, scrolling on his phone.

'Why don't you go to Olivia?' I asked.

I heard the birds chirping softly outside as I waited for Lucien to reply.

'Because there is a limit to how much I can handle being in that house. It doesn't have the happiest memories.'

No, it wasn't a happy home. The state of the house, how orderly it was, always felt like a cell to me rather than a home.

'I have to go to the hospital,' he announced.

'Okay,' I said.

He came closer, and I didn't move. 'Thank you for letting me stay.'

'Um… it's not a problem,' I said. 'I should thank you.'

He lowered his head, but I turned my face away and his lips landed on my cheek. There was an awkward silence before he turned and walked out without saying another word.

#

My phone rang. It was the realtor. He called to inform me that there might be an interested buyer, that they were negotiating on a price and he'd keep me posted.

At last, I thought after I hung up, *some good news*. I tried to get some work done, then I took a small break to make a cup of coffee and a sandwich, and I texted my parents. I tried to call Anna, but she wouldn't take my call. I sent a text to Ben asking him if he could come around.

Later in the afternoon, I got a text from Ben, saying that he'd be around in half an hour and asking if I'd be home. I had to show him that patch of grease in the bathroom and see if he found something else regarding the roses.

Half an hour later, the bell echoed in the house. Ben stood at my doorstep with his hands on his hips, glancing over his shoulder.

'Hi,' I said.

I peered over his shoulder to see what had caught his attention, but nothing was amiss.

'Emily,' he said with a smile.

I opened the door wider for him, and he walked in, glancing around the house. I had managed to clean up the place a bit, and it looked less untidy. I crossed my hands across my chest as I directed him to the living room and offered him a drink.

'I need to head back to the station,' he said.

'I found something in the bathroom. It could be nothing,' I said.

He tilted his head to one side and gave me a look as if to say, *'You always call when something happens.'*

'What did you find?' he asked.

I walked past him, went to the bathroom, and pointed my finger at the shimmery bit. 'I think it's grease.'

He walked into the bathroom and glanced at the floor. 'Did you use grease on something?'

'No, I didn't. I was having a bath and nearly slipped when I noticed it.'

'You think someone came in your house and dropped a few drops of grease. Why would they do that?'

It sounded absurd now hearing him saying it.

'I don't know. I checked the camera and no one has been here.'

'Did you find anything missing?'

'I… don't think so….'

Ben raised an eyebrow. 'You're not sure?'

'I haven't fully checked….'

He walked out of the bathroom and plodded towards the front door.

'You didn't have a handyman come by lately?' he asked, checking the front door.

'No,' I said.

He shut the front door. 'No sign of a break-in.'

'I would have noticed that.'

'Look around the house and see if you find anything missing,' he suggested.

'But aren't you going to take a sample?' I asked.

'Of what?'

'Of the grease.'

He sighed as if to say I had bigger fish to fry.

'First, change the locks, and do you have cameras installed in the house?'

'No.'

'When I told you to install a spy cam, I meant for you to have cameras installed everywhere.'

Heat rose in my cheeks, making me feel like child getting scolded by a parent. I felt foolish and stupid for not doing this.

His phone went off, and he slipped it out of his inner breast pocket and looked at the screen.

'I have to take this,' he said, and accepted the call.

I waited while he talked to whomever was on the line while passing glances at me and whispering to the other person on the line.

'I have to run. I'm needed at the station,' he explained.

He went to the door, and I went after him.

'Is there any news about the roses?'

He turned and glared at me. 'No, I checked with flower shops. There were a few that sell these particular roses.'

'And?'

He checked his watch and rubbed his jaw. 'We are looking into it.'

'We?'

'The other officers. I've heard there was another attack, this time on Lucien's friend, Sasha.'

'Yes, I think it's the same person.'

'I think so, too.'

He opened the door, and it sunk in what he said… Police officers were looking into who had bought those roses. Was there an ongoing investigation?

'Wait…' I said.

'Why are police officers looking into the buyers of these flowers?' I asked.

'We look into all kinds of leads, although I suspect they were home grown rather than store-bought.'

'But why are the police looking into them?'

He threw his head back as if thinking of something. 'I've heard that petals of the Black Baccara rose were found in the place where Sasha was attacked.'

I threw my hand over my mouth.

'I need to go,' he said. 'I'll call you.'

Chapter Thirty-four

Were there rose petals when Anna was attacked? Ben left in such a hurry I couldn't grill him further. People we cared about were being attacked, but why? What was the motivation behind it? I wasn't going to be a prisoner in my own home and let this person run my life. I put on my tweed coat and took out my phone, then typed in Travis's username on Instagram. There was nothing new, though he didn't post much, but the profile picture had a pink circle meaning he had recently posted a story or stories. I was reluctant to press on it, but he wouldn't be able to tell it was me, as I was using a fake profile with a user name of Alisonwhookie_1986, and the profile was a picture of a kitten with no photos. If he did check who saw his story or stories, he would be unable to tell I was the person looking. I clicked on it. The story was a selfie. His pink fringe was brushed sideways, covering his forehead, his blue eyes were piercing, and he was pouting his full lips. 'Hide U' by Kosheen was playing, which he was too young to remember when it was released. I was surprised he knew the song. I put the phone away. These youngsters used quotes or songs to get the message across and hid behind mobile phones instead of saying it face to face. Lucien's account was still disabled, so if this message was to him, he wouldn't be able to see it.

This wasn't part of the plan, but my feet had a life of their own and took me to my old house, as if the answers I was seeking were there. I glanced over my shoulder to Olivia's house. The lights were on, and I could make out the blur of the TV. I glanced back at my house. The 'for sale' sign was still by the front yard and would remain there until a contract was signed. I fiddled with the keys and hurried inside and shut the door before Olivia and Mrs. Parker saw me. There was a smell of enclosed space as I walked around the rooms and went upstairs, not knowing what I was looking for. I went to the back of the house and noticed the back door, which was open. Why was the back door open? I went out into the backyard and buttoned my coat. It was cold, and the wind whipped into the trees. The sky was greying, and winter would soon be among us. I patrolled the yard, but nothing seemed amiss.

Yet I had the impression that someone was coming into this house apart from the realtor. Only the realtor and I had the keys, which I gave him a copy of. Maybe he left it open when he was showing the house? Would someone be that careless? I doubted it because Gary was very professional. He wouldn't leave doors unlocked. I went back inside as a coldness shifted inside me. I checked the door and the lock, but it seemed fine. I did the same with the front door. It also looked untouched. If someone was coming into the house, Mrs. Parker would have called like she did the first time, but she wouldn't be able to see them if they were using the back door. I left the house through the back, made sure the back door was locked and shuffled back to the street. Was someone coming into my house? My mind kept pondering the question as I entered a pub. It wasn't busy, and there was a commentary on the TV showing a replay of a recent football game. I went to the bar where a middle-aged man was arranging the liquor bottle but stopped with his task to serve me. I ordered a gin and tonic and a packet of peanuts. I hadn't eaten anything all day, and I didn't have much appetite, but I needed to get something in my system. I checked my phone, but there were no messages. Someone approached me from behind and stood next to me. I glanced up and did a double take. Jan had his body facing me and a cheeky grin upon his handsome face.

'Emily,' he purred.

'What are you doing here?' I asked.

I couldn't mask the alarm from my voice, and the barman looked at both of us, then back at me before placing my drink and peanuts on the counter.

'Beer, mate,' Jan said, then turned his attention back to me. 'What I'm doing here?' he asked me after the barman had moved away to fill him a pint. 'What are you doing here?'

I lifted the glass of gin to him.

'That's what people do in pubs. They drink,' he said.

'Is that why you're here?'

The barman placed Jan's pint on the counter, and Jan handed him a twenty-pound note and told the barman to cover my tab. Jan ran his hand through his silky black hair and eyed me sharply.

'You don't like me, do you?'

'What gave you that idea?' I asked

'Your hostility.'

'I'm not—'

He lifted an eyebrow at me.

'I don't know you that well,' I said.

He moved closer. 'Maybe you should.'

What was this? This Adonis of a man had a crush on me or something? Lucien lingered at the back of my mind.

I took a sip of my gin. 'Maybe I shouldn't.'

'Why not? Because of Anna? Nothing happened between her and me. How is she? Is she better?'

'Yes, she's getting better,' I said. 'And I don't want to step into dangerous territory.'

He laughed. 'Lucien?'

'Partly.'

'Partly? You think he would care?' he purred.

'Care about what?'

'Never mind,' he said, and took a sip of his beer.

'What do you think of Travis?' I asked.

He placed the glass down with a thud. 'I like him… he's a great company. Why?'

'No reason.'

'I take it Lucien told you, then?'

'Yes, and he told me about Olivia too.'

'He loves you,' Jan said. 'No matter what happens, you're the woman he will keep loving. It's not my place, but you should give him a chance.'

I gulped down more of my gin. 'I don't want to think about that now.'

Jan traced the rim of the glass with his finger. 'His mum was jealous of Olivia.'

I glanced at him. 'Why?'

He shrugged. 'You know his mum.'

'Yeah, I know,' I said.

'Amelia let herself go while Olivia was successful, stylish and kind. She used to take Lucien to visit when he was a child, but then she stopped. Lucien was fond of Olivia, so he kept visiting her.'

'He told me this, and that you used to go along with him. For how long have you known him?'

'Too long. He has always been part of my life.'

'It's good to have someone close to you.'

'Don't you have that?'

'Yes, I do with Anna… but…' I paused to finish my drink. 'I'm going to get another drink. You want anything?'

'No, I should be going,' he said.

'Oh,' I said.

'You sound disappointed,' he remarked.

I stared at him as he gazed down at me. 'You must hear this a lot, but you're absolutely gorgeous.'

He smiled. 'Well, you're not so bad.'

He blew me a kiss, and I watched him walk out of the pub. I turned, facing the barman who was looking at Jan. I ordered another drink and reached for my bag, looking for my wallet. I pushed my hand down to the bottom, but it wasn't there. I took everything out of my bag and my heart sank. I was sure my wallet was there, and I hadn't changed my bag in ages. I cancelled my drink order and left the bar with my mind racing. Maybe it fell off my bag when I left the house. My tube card was in the bag. I had a habit of leaving it in my pockets but not in my wallet. I looked again, but my wallet wasn't there. I took the tube and hurried home. It was growing dark now, and the crickets were singing as I unlocked my front door and searched for my wallet. I looked under the cushions, under the sofa, in drawers, and just in case, even the fridge, not that I would ever place it there.

'Where the fuck is it?' I shouted to the empty house.

Was the house empty? Was it always empty? I retraced my steps, running over each place where I could have used the wallet. Had someone taken it? Lucien had slept on the sofa, so did he go through my bag? Why would he take my wallet? What use did he have for it?

Chapter Thirty-five

By the desk sat a bored-looking police officer who was scribbling down on something, not paying any attention to me. I cleared my throat, and she looked up.

'May I help you, madam?' she asked.

'Yes, I want to report my wallet stolen,' I said.

She returned back to her writing as if this was uninteresting to her. How many people walked in reporting wallets and phones missing?

'When was the last time you had your wallet, madam?' she asked.

'Before I went to the pub,' I said.

She cast me a look. Mentioning a pub wasn't the brightest idea; she must think I was getting pissed and lost my wallet.

'I see,' she said.

Footsteps and voices sounded from the stairs.

'If you could take a seat, I will be back with—'

'Emily?' a familiar voice called out.

I looked up, and Ben stood by the stairs buttoning his jacket. Next to him stood a middle-aged man dressed in a dark suit. Ben said something to the man and then walked over to me.

'I got this,' he said to the officer behind the desk.

I wondered what had happened to his partner, DC Sparks. Ben took me by the arm to a place out of earshot.

'What are you doing here? Are you all right?' he asked.

'I lost my wallet,' I said.

'Can you think of a place you had it last?'

'That's the thing… I always leave it in my bag.'

'Let me write your statement,' he said.

'Thank you, you have been so helpful.'

'It's my pleasure,' he said.

Ben offered to drive me home even though it was the last place I wanted to be.

'Are you still on duty?' I asked as we walked out of the police station.

'No, I'm done for the day.'

'Do you get a day off?'

'Yes, but not a lot, though.'

He opened the door of the silver sedan, and I got in.

'I'm sorry,' I said after he got in and started the car.

'For what?'

'For this. You must think I'm so messed up.'

'I don't think you are.'

'Just a woman who went through traumatic events?'

He looked at me but said nothing.

He drove for a bit, and we stopped at a traffic light. It was fully dark out now, and the lights were glimmering, making the streets sparkle. People walked past, hurrying to go home or out with friends.

'Are you still in touch with that bloke?' he asked.

'What bloke?' I asked.

I knew which bloke he was referring to.

'Lucien Jones.'

'Oh, him,' I said casually. 'We're friendly.'

'You still speak after what happened?' he asked, not hiding the disbelief in his voice.

'We reconnected recently.'

'I see… Weren't you in a relationship with him?'

'I wouldn't call it that.'

'He's… rather odd.'

'Odd?' I asked.

'That's how he appears to me.'

This hung in the air as he drove quietly.

#

Ben pulled over in front of my house, and I looked at my red front door. I could see my steps, but there was nothing there. I removed my seatbelt and looked at Ben.

'Thank you,' I said.

'It's not a problem.'

'Would you….' I paused, unsure if I should finish my question.

Ben waited for me to elaborate.

'Like to come in?' I offered. 'If you don't have any plans, of course.'

'No, I was going to go home and watch TV. I could have a drink.'

He killed the engine, removed his seatbelt, and we walked to my house side by side. I unlocked the door, but Ben stopped me and said he would go in first while I stayed where I was. I waited while he checked and then reappeared at the front door.

'Sorry about that,' he said. 'Had to make sure.'

I nodded in response, and I went to the kitchen and offered him a drink. He asked for beer, which I didn't have, and instead opted for wine.

'You told me the other day,' I began, 'that rose petals were found where Sasha was attacked.'

'Yes,' he said.

'Were there rose petals when Anna was attacked?'

'No, but as I said, they are looking at both cases, as they think they are linked.'

I wanted to ask if they had a suspect, but I didn't want him to think I invited him there to grill him with questions. Really it was because I didn't want to be alone in the house, at least for a while, and I liked him.

'What ever happened to your partner, DC Sparks?' I asked as I took a step closer to him.

He peered at me. 'He was transferred.'

'Oh, and you don't have a partner now?'

'We come in pairs like a set of earrings.'

'Was the gentleman you were speaking to at the stairs your new partner?' I asked.

'No, my partner is a woman now. She's very tough.'

'Oh, is she?'

'That's what I said.'

I curled my hand to his jacket. 'And you like tough women?'

He took a sip of wine and placed it down on the counter without taking his eyes off me. His expression was a mix of seriousness and amusement.

'That depends.'

I moved in closer, not knowing what was getting into me, but I wanted to have that moment. To be with someone. To feel something. I kissed him gently at first, then he parted my mouth with his tongue and we fell into one another. I peeled his jacket off and let it drop on the floor. We manoeuvred our way through my tiny house, tearing at our clothes, and finally made it to the bedroom.

Chapter Thirty-six

I woke up the next morning with the sun blazing in my eyes. I groaned and turned to the other side of the bed, where Ben was asleep beside me. I sat up straight, looking around the bedroom to see clothes were scattered on the floor. I rubbed my face with the palms of my hands as the memories of the previous evening came flooding back. Sleeping with Ben would complicate things, and deep down, I felt I was being disloyal to Lucien, which was ridiculous. I didn't owe him anything. The floor was cold under my bare feet as I reached for my old, oversized T-shirt, and Ben stirred at the movement.

'Hey,' he said.

'Hi,' I said.

'What time is it?'

I checked the time on my phone. 'A little after eight.'

He rubbed his eyes. 'I need to be at the station in an hour.'

'Would you like a cup of coffee before you go?'

'That would be lovely,' he said.

I made my way out of the bedroom and went to the kitchen. Ben's wine glass was still on the counter, half-finished and warm. I emptied it in the sink, placed the bottle next to the bin, and put the kettle on. In the living room, Ben's jacket lay on the floor. I picked it up, dusted it off, and his wallet fell out. I was going to slide it back in the jacket pocket, but something inside nagged at me. No, I shouldn't, I wouldn't, but all that had happened to me made me wary and distrustful of people. I glanced back at the bedroom, to where I could hear Ben moving around but couldn't see him. His phone rang, and he picked it up right away. I took the chance to open the wallet. Inside, there was cash, business cards, credit cards, his driving licence and ID. His badge wasn't there, but he would likely keep it in another pocket. I buried my hand in one of the wallet compartments and slipped out a photo.

I glanced over my shoulder and saw Ben was still talking on the phone. The photo was taken in a pub and two pints were on the table. Beside Ben sat a smiley blonde woman. I frowned. Ben said he didn't have time for relationships. Then who was this woman? An ex-girlfriend? But why would anyone carry a photo of their ex in their wallet? Was she a sister? Ben hung up, and I put the picture back and slipped the wallet inside, then placed the jacket on the sofa as the kettle started to boil. I made the coffees as Ben came out. As he put on his blazer, I handed him a mug of coffee. I couldn't ask him about the woman, as I would expose that I had been prying, which wouldn't go down well. We talked for a bit, mostly about our plans for the day. After he finished his coffee, Ben announced he had to go. I walked him to the door, and he kissed me on the lips. Then I watched him get into his car and drive off. I was about to close the door when I saw Lucien approaching the house, and heat scorched my body up to my face. Did he see Ben leave the house?

'Hey,' he said, looking me up and down.

I had forgotten I was only dressed in a T-shirt.

'Is this a good time?'

I detected a slight tension in his tone. He had seen Ben. Of course, he did. How could he miss him when Lucien had a cat's alertness, but why should he care? I nodded, and the guilt swept through me, which was silly. He followed me inside the house and scanned it, probably trying to guess where the act had happened. On the sofa? The floor? The chair? By the wall? I went to the bedroom and shut the door. I put on a pair of leggings and made the bed quickly, covering all traces of sex with the duvet. I felt like one of those guilty wives who was concealing evidence of her deception. Jan's words drifted into my consciousness… *'He loves you no matter what happens. You're the woman he will keep on loving.'*

Lucien was sitting on the sofa with his long legs propped up on the coffee table. I glanced at his laced-up boots for no reason, then went to the kitchen and put the kettle on again.

'Sasha will be released from the hospital this afternoon,' he announced.

The air in the house felt thick, and my chest hurt.

'That's good news,' I said.

'Yeah, she'll be staying at her parents' until she gets better.'

'Where do her parents live?' I asked

'Dorset,' he said.

'That's a lovely place.'

'You've been?'

'Yes, once a long time ago. Have you been?'

'No, never been,' he said.

I made another mug of coffee.

'I ran into Jan in a pub,' I announced.

'You did?'

I turned, and he was leaning against the door frame. He moved with silence. Lucien did not just have the alertness of a cat, but also the stealth of one.

'Yes, we talked.'

'About me?' he asked.

I stirred the coffee with a teaspoon. 'Your name did come up.'

He glared at me, and without saying anything, he walked out of the kitchen. I followed him and saw he was putting his coat back on.

'You're leaving?' I asked.

He turned. 'Why? Do you want me to stay?'

'What are you doing here?'

'I came to check up on you, but you have it all under control, don't you, Emily?'

'Have what under control?'

'Oh please, I saw him leave your house.'

'So? What is the issue? You have open relationships and shag whomever you like. You're a big boy, so why are you being like this?'

'Because I'm fucking jealous, that's why!' he shouted.

I crossed my arms under my chest. 'I'm not going to justify myself to you.'

'Doesn't matter,' he said and lowered his head. Then he started towards the door and stopped.

'I love you, Emily, I always did, but with all that has happened….' He sighed, as if having difficulty translating his feelings into words. 'Never mind.'

'Sometimes love is not enough,' I said.

He looked at me as if I slapped him, then he turned to the door and left.

Chapter Thirty-seven

I sat in the coffee shop in Berkeley Square with a cappuccino in front of me as I admired the sunny view from the window, watching as people meandered by. The door of the coffee shop opened, and Anna walked in. She was wearing an animal-print coat and smart trousers, and her face had healed entirely. Although she looked herself, the experience would live on in her memories. She placed the bag on the empty chair and sat across from me. She had called the previous day requesting me to meet her here, and I dropped everything to see her.

'Thank you for reaching out,' I said.

'You're my friend. I wouldn't abandon you. I just needed some time to process what you told me.'

'I'm sorry I didn't tell you sooner. I just didn't want to worry you.'

'I know,' she said.

A waitress walked past, and Anna ordered tea from her.

'So, how have you been?' I asked.

'I'm slowly getting past it… The police came to ask me more questions. They suspect that my attack and Sasha's are linked.'

'Ben told me they found rose petals where she got attacked. Did they say if there were any rose petals where you were…?' I paused, looking for the right word, but was there any.

'No,' Anna said. 'They didn't mention anything about rose petals. Have you gotten any more flowers?'

'No.'

'What does it all mean?' she asked.

'I wish I knew.'

'Anyway,' she said. 'Let's talk about something else. How have you been?'

'I ran into Jan in a pub.'

'I know,' she said.

My eyes widened. 'You know? How?'

'He reached out on Facebook, and he apologised for everything. We have been chatting and he asked me to meet up, but I need more time.'

'You should focus on yourself first,' I suggested.

'That's what I intend to do.'

I nodded. 'I lost my wallet, by the way.'

'Oh, where?'

'I don't know… It was in my bag, and then it was gone.'

'You think you got robbed?' she asked.

'I don't know… I had to cancel all of my cards and get a new ID.' I sighed. 'It's all an inconvenience.'

The waitress served Anna her tea.

'Did you report it?' Anna asked after the waitress had walked off.

'Yes, Ben took a statement.'

She reached for the sugar. 'Ben? So, you're still seeing him?'

I glanced at the window as what transpired between us came flooding back. 'Yes….'

'I think he would be good for you.'

I thought of the picture in his wallet. *Who was that woman?*

'I don't want a relationship,' I confessed.

She stirred her tea. 'You can still meet up and be casual.'

'And look how brilliantly that turned out,' I said.

She stared at me. 'What do you mean?'

'Lucien.'

The image of how hurt he looked came before me, and I took a sip of my coffee to distract myself.

'Ah, well… I don't want to overstep, but I think you should cut all ties with him. He's not a good influence.'

All the bad things that had happened to me were because of him, and somehow, I had the growing suspicion that this was related to him. I was working my head around why.

'He loves me….' I confessed.

Her face hardened. 'Oh, Emily. You're in big trouble.'

'What do you mean?' I asked.

'It's messy.'

'Yes, and I don't want to think about nor deal with it.'

'Do you love him?' Anna asked.

I ran my clammy hands on my jeans. *Do I love Lucien?* I did find him incredibly beautiful, and I still desired him, but desire wasn't equivalent to love.

#

I was about to go in the house when a silver sedan pulled over in front of my house and Ben came out buttoning his suit jacket. He smiled at me, and I smiled at him as I let him in.

Ben had his body close to mine, running his hand on my thigh and kissing my shoulder as I watched the curtain move gently with the breeze. The motion drew my eyes to my furniture, and I noticed it needed dusting. *Why do we bother to dust the furniture when it just comes back?*

'This was unexpected,' I said.

'I wanted to surprise you,' he said.

'What if I had a man?' I asked, and Lucien's face appeared in my vision. Young with a tight body so youthful and full of life. I envied the freedom he possessed, the innocence that he could be anything, yet also mysterious and now tragic.

'I would have been very jealous,' Ben said, snapping me out of my thoughts of the other man.

Both Ben and Lucien floated in my life like that angry storm that wouldn't leave me alone. Both were jealous men. What stunned me was that I wouldn't have taken Lucien as the jealous type. He was so open about his sexuality, so laid back, and I kept asking myself, why me? There was a city of beautiful men and women who would die to be with him. What was I to him?

'Do you have any brothers or sisters?' I asked, thinking of the woman in the picture.

'No, an only child. You?'

'I'm an only child,' I said.

If that woman wasn't his sister, then who was she?

Chapter Thirty-eight

Ben didn't own any social media accounts, and he was only briefly mentioned in a few news articles, so I was left with a dead end when I searched for him online. I looked in the news to see if any other women were getting attacked that might lead to something, but there was nothing. I closed the tabs and went back to work.

Ben came over again, and I wanted to ask him about the woman in the picture. She had held enough significance in his life to carry her photo with him. *Was she a girlfriend who passed away in tragic circumstances?* I couldn't ask him because he would know I went through his wallet. After our time together, I watched him get dressed.

'Back to work?' I asked.

'Back to work,' he repeated.

'You want to maybe go out for dinner sometime?'

'Sure, I'll keep you posted.'

He left shortly after that, and I changed the sheets and threw the dirty ones in the washing machine. Another question popped into my mind. *Why didn't he invite me over to his place?* I went back to work, and Olivia texted me to meet up for dinner. I knew what this meant. She wanted a progress report. I wondered if Lucien had told her that I knew who she was. I agreed to meet her the next evening when she suggested a restaurant in Mayfair.

#

As I suspected, the restaurant was high-class. It had a stained-glass ceiling and a red fitted carpet, and the tables' legs were gilded with gold and topped with blue silk tablecloths. The lights were turned down low, making the place look intimate and romantic. A little too much for two friends meeting for a business dinner. Were Olivia and I friends? A snooty hostess with six-inch-high heels guided me to the table where Olivia was sipping a glass of champagne. She stood when I approached, and we air-kissed as the hostess placed the menus on the table and then walked off. Olivia was dressed in a black dress with a floral puffed skirt. It was a dress suited more for a wedding than for dinner. This woman kept choosing places where I had to remove my comfy sweatpants and make an effort.

'You look ravishing in red. It suits you,' Olivia said when we sat down.

'Thank you,' I said.

'So, how are you? It seems like ages since we last spoke.'

'I'm good,' I said. 'I started working on your pieces and—'

She rose her hand. 'This is not a business dinner. I just wanted to catch up and have a little bit of fun – wine and dine.'

Olivia sure did know how to wine and dine. She ordered the wine with the passing waiter while I scowled at the menu.

'So, how is Lucien?' she asked after placing her order with the waiter.

I was taken aback by this question. Did she know that I knew? It would be an interesting conversation to have.

'I haven't seen him,' I said.

'Oh, why?' she asked.

The waiter arrived with the wine, and I was relieved for the brief interlude. It would buy me time to think about how to answer her question. I thought this was a business dinner where I would share ideas with her, not talk about Lucien. It would have been better if we had talked about work. After the waiter made a big show of pouring the wine, Olivia turned her attention back to me.

I took a sip of wine. 'I'm busy with work.'

'He told me that he told you about me.'

'Oh,' I said.

'Did it surprise you?'

'Well….' I stalled and took another sip of the crisp, fruity wine. 'You do look similar.'

'Amelia and I have a complicated relationship. She was resentful… envied me. But nothing was stopping her from having the same life as mine.'

'Do you think she set the bakery on fire?'

Amelia worked at her parents' bakery, which had caught fire under mysterious circumstances. She told me that she closed the business because she was pregnant with Sylvian at the time and wanted to stay at home and look after him, but I found out from Mrs. Parker there had been a fire.

'There was no proof she had done it, but it wouldn't surprise me after all she has done. I didn't see the children much during this time. Amelia had always been possessive and prevented me from having a relationship with them.'

'Have you ever been in the house in Exeter?' I asked.

She took a large gulp of wine. 'No.'

'I have.'

'Oh,' she said, surprised about this.

'Lucien took me on the anniversary of his brother's….'

'I had no idea you were that close,' she said.

I played with the spoon. 'We're not that… close.'

'No?' she asked, with one eyebrow raised. 'Yet he shared that part of himself with you, taking you to that house. He never did that with anyone. You were close and he trusts you.'

I didn't know what to say to this, so I gulped down more wine.

'He ran away from home after the disappearance,' Olivia confessed.

I swallowed hard. 'Lucien ran away from home?'

He never mentioned this to me, but he wouldn't tell me everything even if he trusted me.

'Yes, he came to stay with me. He never told you about this?'

'No.'

'It was a stressful time. He was sick that night, but he heard voices outside his bedroom window and thought he was dreaming. It still haunts him. He recently told me he should have known the voices were real and the bedroom led directly to the well. That he should have known his brother was down there. He feels guilty about it.'

'But it's not his fault. How could he have known?'

'Henry and Amelia came to pick him up,' Olivia continued. 'Amelia alleged that I was poisoning Lucien against them while Henry stayed in the background saying nothing.'

'Were you?' I asked.

Another waiter walked over to tell us the specials.

Olivia lifted her hand at him. 'Not now,' she said with an authoritative tone. I pictured her dismissing her staff with a snap of a finger.

'No, Emily,' she said after the red-faced waiter stomped off. 'Amelia and I had our differences, but I would never do that. He kept coming to see me without her knowledge.'

'You knew Henry wasn't his father?'

'No, but I had my suspicions. Sylvian and Lucien looked nothing alike. Sylvian had taken a lot after Henry. He was a handsome boy, Sylvian. It always made me wonder, well… there are a lot of brothers and sisters who look nothing alike. Nothing

Lucien did pleased Henry. Lucien used to ask me why Henry hated him? Why couldn't he love him?'

According to Amelia, Henry knew the moment Lucien was born that he wasn't his. How he knew was beyond me, but I think a father would know. He wanted to leave Amelia, but she threatened him with his career in the army, and he had no choice but to stay. Henry knew even right then what she was capable of. It was hard for me to sympathise with Henry, though. He was so unlikeable, and taking out his anger and resentment on a child – that was unacceptable in my books. Lucien was blameless in all of that. If Henry had to take it out on someone, he should have done that on Amelia.

'Do you know who his father is?' I asked.

'No, she wouldn't tell me she had a fling with another man while her husband was serving his country.' Olivia opened the menu and dropped the subject. 'We should order.'

I knew that the conversation about Lucien was over for the rest of the evening.

I arrived home a little after ten, and from the Uber, I saw a woman sitting on the step of my house. I contemplated telling the driver to keep driving, but she looked up and my heart sank as I recognised who she was. The woman from the picture in Ben's wallet.

Chapter Thirty-nine

I had gotten myself in messy situations that were beyond my control, but I had no idea about this. I should have known, however, that Ben was lying to me. The night was quiet and most of the houses were in darkness as the street lamps cast an orange glow. The woman stood and stomped towards me, her face a Kabuki mask of anger.

'You're Emily Clarke?' she asked, sizing me up. 'Of course, you are,' she snarled. 'Do you know who I am?'

My tongue grew too fat to speak, so I shook my head.

'I'm his wife!'

His wife? Ben was married? It all started to make sense, yet it still shocked me. Ben never wore a ring, but rings could be taken off.

'He didn't tell me he was married,' I managed to say.

'Is that your excuse?' she shouted.

I glanced around the neighbourhood. I didn't want a scene.

'I didn't know....' My voice disappeared.

She took another step closer, but I stayed where I was. So much for the smiley blonde in the picture, but I couldn't expect her to be pleasant under these circumstances. I would do the same if I were in her shoes. I tried to rationalise the situation – Ben was married, but he didn't tell me. I felt cheated, betrayed, and humiliated. As if I hadn't been through enough, this was the last thing I needed. What was Ben thinking? Why get me involved in this? How could I allow myself to be this foolish? He didn't behave like a man who was married. But how did a married man behave? My mind went back to all the times I had met up with him, trying to detect a sign of deception. I thought of his answers and how vague they were, and then the whispering on the phone. That should have been a giveaway. I noticed she was holding something in her hand – an envelope. I swallowed the lump that hung in my throat, choking me. She shoved the envelope into my chest.

'You fucking slag!' she shouted.

My next-door neighbour's light went on, and my body trembled. I moved past her as tears smeared down my face.

'This is on your head!' she yelled after me. 'Hope you're happy that you just ruined a marriage!'

#

I hid from the world under the covers, too broken to move. I didn't know what time it was or what day, and I didn't care. I tried to reason that it wasn't my fault. I didn't know. Ben did. Yet never had I felt so dirty and so ashamed. The envelope his wife had shoved at me was proof of my 'crime.' Filthy and deceitful. Where did she get the photos from? Maybe she had been suspicious of her husband and hired a P.I. It would make perfect sense. I would never intentionally do that to another woman; I wasn't a thief. I had been cheated on by Ed, so I knew how it felt. Men. Parasites. Leeches who take and take until they suck you dry. Hyenas. I was done with their shit and their drama.

After I didn't know for how long, I managed to get out of bed, dragged myself to the kitchen and poured myself a glass of wine. The photographs were still on the counter. I had left them there when I rushed to the toilet to vomit all the wine and food I had consumed with Olivia. The photo displayed Ben coming into my house, my head appearing slightly. I grabbed them and threw them in the bin. I went to the bathroom and had a long bath, thinking of nothing. Afterward, I returned to my desk. A dog barked in the distance, and the rain trickled gently against the windows. I booted up my laptop and poured myself another glass of wine. What a great time to try to ease my drinking. Fifty emails were waiting to be read, and the idea of reading and replying to them one by one made me want to throw myself out of the window. I thought I would do a design on Canva instead. I wasn't in the right state of mind to write material, but I could deal with designs for Facebook ads. That, at least, would keep me occupied, because I had been sleeping for days. I scrolled through my pictures. There was so much junk there, I should delete most of it. An image flew past, and I scrolled up and enlarged it. It was one of the images I had saved of Lucien. He was standing by a bed of long leaves and dressed in a beautiful organza blouse. I had forgotten I had saved it. I stood from the desk, searching for my phone and finding it under the sofa with the battery screaming that it was down to five percent. I put the phone on to charge as I glanced at the notifications. There were fifteen missed calls and six text messages. I went through the texts first. There were four from Ben. I deleted them without reading them and blocked his number. I wasn't interested in what he had to say. He deceived me and made me look like a fool. There was a text from Mum and another from Anna. The missed calls were from clients, which made me roll my eyes. I poured more wine and glanced at the photo of Lucien, still on the screen as he stared back at me. I groaned and closed the tab, as if this somehow would banish him from my thoughts.

#

The doorbell went off, but I was reluctant to answer the door. I ignored it as I turned to the other side of the bed. My phone rang shortly after, and I reached for it out of curiosity.

'Are you home?' Anna asked. 'I'm at your door.'

I mustered all of my energy to get up from the bed to make it to the door. Anna stood before me dressed in her work attire – a smart suit with a tote bag dangling from her arm. She looked poised and elegant, a woman who wouldn't let what had happened to her define her.

'My god,' she said. 'What happened to you?'

Without saying anything, I moved away and let her deal with the door. Her heels clicked on the floor while I shuffled into the kitchen and put the kettle on. I was in pyjamas, and there were dark circles under my eyes. I knew I looked terrible.

'This place is a mess,' she complained. 'And it smells like something has died here.'

I heard her open a window. 'Do you have something against light?'

'Anna, please,' I cried.

She appeared in the kitchen. 'What's happened to you?'

'Do you really want to know?' I asked her.

'Yes,' she said, walking over. 'Let me take care of this. Go and sit down.'

She made the tea and opened the fridge, looking for the milk. When she grabbed it, she sniffed at the carton and pulled a face.

'You need to get your shit in order and sort out this fridge! You're not like this.'

She pushed the pedal of the bin with her shoe and threw the carton inside. I caught a glimpse of the envelope, but I didn't think she had noticed it. Anna placed the two mugs of black tea on the table and sat across from me.

'Is it Lucien?' she asked.

I shook my head. What made her think it was him? He had done nothing wrong, and despite everything, he was one of the few people who wouldn't deceive me, at least not like Ben had. I broke down then, and she took me into her arms.

'I'll kill him!' Anna said after I finished telling her what had happened. 'How dare he do that to you after what you have been through. What a knob!'

'What I can say?' I said, wiping the tears with my fingers and sniffing. 'I attract them.'

Her eyes went wide. 'Oh my God, and I encouraged you. I'm partly responsible.'

'You didn't know. He had us fooled.'

'How did his wife find out?'

I hesitated, then pointed my finger at the bin. She glanced back at it as if it were a bomb, then stood and pulled out the photos. I watched as her eyes widened with shock with each flip, and she placed her hand over her mouth.

'I think she hired a private investigator,' I explained

Anna placed the photos back in the bin and came to the sofa. We sipped our tea in silence.

'Are you sure she hired a private investigator?' Anna asked.

'Is there any other explanation?'

'What if the person who sent you the roses also sent those to his wife?'

Chapter Forty

It was like a swarm of ants made their way from my collar to my hair. Was it true? Was Anna right? Did the person who sent me the roses send those photos to Ben's wife? How did they manage to capture those photos? That wouldn't be too hard, not with what technology offered nowadays. Were they hiding behind the bushes when they took the photos?

Anna offered for me to stay with her until the 'craziness died down.' It wasn't going to die down, though. Someone was out there stalking me, watching my every move. They knew how I spent my days, the people I met with, and what I did. I couldn't even shit in peace. I assured Anna it would be fine. She seemed hesitant to leave but promised me she would call. After she left, I went to the kitchen, opened the bin, and removed the photos. I didn't know what use I had for them. To see myself in those photos like that without loathing myself. But throwing them away wasn't a bright idea. I sent an email to my clients that I was going to take a few days off. Although she understood, I could sense Olivia's prickliness, but I didn't care what she thought. I made sure the camera was working, and a thought came to me. This person, whoever it was, knew I had a camera and was using other methods to get to me. I checked all the windows, ensured they were secure, and locked the front door.

The sky had taken on a shade of pink and blue with a hint of orange. It was the kind of sky you had to stop and take a photo of, then post it on Instagram and use a quote as a caption. The Uber had arrived, and I got in. I could have sent a text, but somehow, I wanted to catch him off guard. The suspicion had prickled into my skin and into my senses. After I got out of the Uber, I glanced up at the block of modern, glassed apartments, and I saw the balcony had people outside, their chatter and laughter whispering with the wind. *Great*, I thought, *they have guests*. A couple, dressed in long leather coats and laced boots with rubber heels, and the girl's arm linked with her companion's, approached the street. Judging from their opulent appearance, they were heading up to their apartment. I pretended to shuffle through my bag while the couple rang the buzzer, and there was the clunk of the communal door. The couple proceeded inside, and the man placed his hand on the small of his escort's back. I followed them inside, but they didn't bother to glance over their shoulders to make sure the door was properly shut. They called for the lift, went inside, and I followed them. The woman's face was heavily made up and the man looked polished, and I wondered what I must look like in their eyes. I was dressed in a black-and-red-checked jacket, with grubby, oversized jeans and trainers that needed a good scrub. I wasn't wearing any makeup, and my hair needed a good wash. I was sure I looked scruffy and dirty in their eyes. Their perfume wafted in the lift, which made the air thick. They didn't speak as we went up to the sixth floor. I let them go out first and waited until the lift was about to close, then I put my hand on it, and it opened again so I could peek through. The couple stood by the door, and music could be heard from the corridor. I took big steps towards the door where the elegant couple had disappeared inside. The door was ajar as I pulled it open and was engulfed by Fat Boy Slim pumping on a JBL speaker. The music wasn't something I was expecting when the room was filled with people cloaked in black clothing, colourful hairstyles and exotic jewellery. I tucked into my jacket, feeling self-conscious and out of place. The apartment was also opulent and decorated with eighteenth-century furniture. The fabrics had patterns of black and gold, chandeliers hung on the ceiling and Persian rugs embellished the floors. I peered past the sofa and made out Lucien having a deep conversation with a girl dressed in what looked like a black sundress with boots that went up to the knee. Her hair was bright orange, and her enormous bosom was about to spill out of her dress. She leaned over Lucien, whose hair was now back to platinum blonde. He looked infinitely stunning. Lucien was smiling at the girl, appearing smitten with her. From the corner of my eyes, I made out a head with pink hair. It was Travis. My eyes went back to Lucien as Travis slumped next to Lucien and put his arm around him, as if he was competing with the girl. I rubbed my forehead. So, they were back together, but Lucien was flirting with the girl in front of Travis? I couldn't understand it nor keep up with it, and I didn't want to. I looked for Jan, but he didn't seem to be anywhere. Lucien was talking to Travis, and his eyes averted in my direction and he did a double take. His mouth gaped open and passed a glance at Travis. I tried to fade into the background and went towards the fireplace, which had a photo of Jan above it. He had his legs tucked under him, all dressed in black, and he was wearing lots of jewellery. His black hair was swept to one side, his eyes gazing seductively at the camera. Who would hang a portrait of themselves on their wall? Models, I supposed. Lucien was coming towards me, his face contoured with confusion, and he looked displeased that I had the audacity to barge in like this while he was hosting guests. Without saying a word, he took my hand and I let him guide me along to where he opened a grey door. We went inside, and he shut the door firmly behind us without turning on the light.

Chapter Forty-one

The gleam from the neighbouring apartments shined through the window. Lucien turned on the light, and the sudden brightness made me shut my eyes. I was in a bedroom with black furniture, a chandelier hanging from the ceiling and a dark purple duvet thrown over a king-sized bed. It was his bedroom, and his boyfriend and girlfriend, or whatever they were, were out there just a room away. I had stepped into dangerous territory here.

'What are you doing here, Emily?' he asked. 'You should have texted. You can't just barge in….' He sighed, then ran his hands through his hair and moved past me.

'I wanted to see you,' I said.

He sat on the bed and looked at me with dispassion. 'I see.'

He was incredulous, but how could I blame him? It was selfish of me to go there unannounced when he had professed his love and I slammed it back in his face. I didn't think Lucien was used to rejection. He might have experienced it a time or two, but not a lot, and too much had happened to repair the damage. As I watched him sitting on the bed with his legs crossed, I wanted to ask him if it was he who sent the photos to Ben's wife. Did Lucien know Ben was married and he neglected to tell me, then let me face the humiliation? Lucien had been clear about his jealousy, and jealousy made people behave irrationally.

'You're back with Travis?' I asked.

He threw his head back and I thought he was going to laugh, but he didn't.

'Why do you want to see me, Emily? What do you want?'

'I... afraid....'

His face softened with this, but he didn't give me a reply.

'Did something strange happen?' I asked.

'Strange?'

'Did you get more roses or something?'

'No. Why, have you?'

I stomped to the bed and sat next to him. 'Ben is married.'

'*What?*'

'Yes, his wife came to the house and started shouting at me, and—'

'Ben is married?' he asked in disbelief.

'Yep, he forgot to share that fact with me.'

'But you never spotted a wedding ring?'

Despite what he had been through and the things he did – the lifestyle that baffled me – right then, he sounded innocent and naive.

'Rings can be taken off.'

There was a hard knock on the door, which made us jump.

'Lucien! Are you in there?'

It was Travis. Lucien sighed with annoyance. I was not sure if this reaction was targeted at Travis for interrupting or at me, not that there was anything to intrude upon. Lucien stood from the bed, walked over to the door and opened it, but not entirely as if to hide the fact that I was there. A rush of music entered the bedroom. Why did Lucien, who was so sexually liberated and had open relationships, hide the fact that I was there?

'I'll be out in a minute,' Lucien said.

'Well, can I come in?' Travis demanded.

'I just need to make a call. I'll be there soon,' Lucien said, and he shut the door in Travis's face.

Lucien turned, scratching his head. 'This is not a good time.'

I stood. 'Of course, I'm sorry to waltz in like this….'

'Go to the house, and I'll come to you when this is over.'

I nodded.

'It's best if I go out first,' he suggested. 'Wait a bit, then come out.'

Lucien was perturbed about something, and without saying anything else, he walked out of the room, where music surged again and then faded once the door was shut. I glanced around the bedroom and an evil thought came to me. *No, I shouldn't*. I couldn't do this again – go around and poke my nose in stuff that didn't concern me. Someone was out there making my life a living hell, and I had to find out if he was connected, even if it would destroy me. The music had changed to Depeche Mode. I hummed to the song as I walked over to the beautiful black dresser. A beautiful room for a beautiful boy. A gilded cage just like his parents' house had been. I pulled open the first drawer, looking for a hidden compartment like in movies. I had taken on a new persona as I searched among his things looking for a skeleton in the closet. He owned a lot of clothes, all elegant and expensive. Clothes and jewellery were everywhere. I looked under the bed, but I was greeted with a polished floor. Did he clean the room himself or hire a maid? The room was immaculate and spotless like his parents' house had been. I imagined he picked up a few traits from Henry. Siouxsie and the Banshees played next, from before my time, let alone theirs. Another artist, aside from Blondie, my mum loved. I flung open the closet, and I looked among the coats and shirts and boots. Nothing. Did he share this room with Travis? Or did Travis have a separate room? I had to stop before he came in and caught me, kicked me out, and never spoke to me again. Voices and laughter blended into one with the music. I walked towards the door as the shame flooded over me. What was I doing looking at his things? This was Lucien. An eager, sweet guy who had helped me when Ed hit me. I stumbled out of the room, legs wobbly, eyes glaring, and the music enveloped me. More people had gathered in the living room, all well-groomed and pretty. I made out Lucien sitting on the sofa where the redhead was about to straddle him.

I manoeuvred my way to the guests. Some were talking, others dancing, but all were dressed in black or purple. Travis was leaning against the wall, and I followed what he was looking at. Lucien, of course, where the redhead had her arms flung around him in an embrace and was looking at him as if she couldn't believe she could get this lucky. Travis looked away, his face dark. What was their relationship about? Who would do that to someone? Either you want to be with someone or you don't. It is that simple. No point in taunting them or wasting their time. Travis spotted me, and his mouth parted slightly, obviously not happy with me being there. He had warned me to stay away, and there I was, disregarding that warning and invading his territory.

Chapter Forty-two

I was jittery, functioning with raw nerves as I paced in the living room, checking the time every now and then. I poured a glass of wine and sat on the sofa with the TV on. Hours passed, and I began to think he wasn't coming. Why should he? He was probably showing that redhead a good time while Travis lingered and pouted, and a small part of me felt sorry for him. To be with someone so glorious but who wouldn't fully commit to you. Who would never be yours. To be that desperate to hold onto something, too afraid to let it go, it was like having everything and nothing at the same time. I dismissed that sympathy away; this was the guy who followed me and told me to stay away. I glanced up from my laptop to rest my heavy eyes and looked at the clock. It was past midnight. I stood to stretch, then went to the kitchen and poured myself another glass of wine. I thought of the person I used to be before all of this, before I moved to this house, before all of this mess. I was someone who had a smile on my face and had a positive outlook on life. An optimist, some would say. I was chatty and bubbly, loud, and always up for a laugh. Now, I didn't recognise that person any more. I had become invisible, found it hard to initiate a conversation, and people turned away from me. Trauma and pain did that to a person. Pain also made me seek solace in the bottle. I took a sip of wine. It was something cheap bought from the supermarket, but I would knock it back anyway. A car rumbled by, and a door slammed shut. Someone must have arrived home, probably one of the teenage daughters from number twenty. Then a knock came at the door, and my phone glowed on my desk, casting a blue light.

Lucien shut the door behind him and glanced down at me. I tried to detect drunkenness, but there didn't seem to be any. He was used to all that partying. I moved away and reached for my glass of wine, hiding the guilt of what I had done in his bedroom, looking into his things like a crazy person. Mistrust was an ugly thing.

'Party over?' I asked.

'No, I snuck out,' he replied.

Like all the beds he had snuck out of in the middle of the night.

'What did Travis think of that?'

Lucien sighed heavily. 'He just lives there.'

Sharing a flat with his ex-lover must be uncomfortable and awkward. To see him bringing other people home. From what I saw, though, Travis still had feelings for him. If I were Travis, I would have moved out the moment the relationship had been terminated. Why put myself through all that pain? But what did I know? I might have been the older one, but I knew nothing. I saw things as black and white, boring with no colour or substance. Ancient. Old fashioned.

'How does that work?' I asked.

'What do you mean how does that work?' he asked, bemused. 'We were in a relationship. Now we're not, and he needs a place to stay. I can't just throw him out, and it is not in my power to do so. It's Jan's apartment, after all.'

I thought of that portrait hanging above the fireplace of gorgeous Jan. *I'm the king of this domain,* that picture seemed to say. In years to come, when Jan grew older and his looks faded, he would look at that picture and say to himself, *This is who I was. How fabulous was I?*

One moment we were in a relationship, but now we're not. I couldn't help but marvel at his mentality and how remarkable he was. Travis, the dismissed. Lucien came to me, reached for the glass of wine, turned the glass over, and drank from the same spot my lips had touched. He licked his lips and placed the glass down.

'Who was the redhead?' I asked.

He sighed at my jealousy-fuelled question. *Why leave a great party to be with a grubby woman who was falling apart and was old and grey? But he loved me. Wasn't I lucky?*

'She's a friend. What is this? Are you jealous, Emily?'

A friend who straddled him and looked at him as if she had won the lottery. A friend, yeah right. Who did he think he was fooling?

'Did you sleep with her?'

'Yes.'

The honesty of it… how easily he rolled out that 'yes.'

'So, she's a friend with benefits?'

I could see the girl with her pale skin, long flaming hair, and that ample bosom, riding him with her eyes closed and her full lips parted with pleasure. *Why was I doing this to myself? What was wrong with me? What he was doing to me?*

'Whatever, Emily, is this how it's going to play out? You interrogating me?'

'I'm sorry,' I said.

I attempted to move away from him, but he grabbed me and took me into his arms.

'None of those relationships are real,' he said.

I turned away from him, but he came close again and wrapped his hands around my waist. Then I felt his breath hot against my ear. 'I remember all of them, every one of them. I think about those moments we spent together. I think about it all the time. It's all I think about. It's all I want.'

'I remember them too, but we discussed this.'

'No,' he whispered. 'You discussed, and you dismissed me.'

'Lucien, please….'

He nuzzled my neck the way he knew I loved, but now I couldn't help associating it with the other people he had slept with. Sasha. Julie. Travis. The redhead. The people before them who were faceless, but we had him in common. All conquests. Yet something inside me twitched and I was weak against his power, and I hated myself for it. My hand reached for him as we kissed, and I turned to him, burying my lips, parting his mouth with my tongue. I sensed his impatience and eagerness as he picked me up and leaned me against the wall like how it was the first time between us.

'It's you I want,' he whispered. 'Nobody else but you.'

He kissed me in a such a way it left me breathless, then pulled me away from the wall and took us to the bedroom.

Chapter Forty-three

The phone screeched as I groaned into the pillow. It was still dark out as my hands fumbled for the phone. I sat up and noticed the other side of the bed was empty. I ran my hand on it, and it was cold. Where was Lucien? Had he left? I pressed the phone to my ear, then bile rose from my stomach and the room blurred.

When I arrived at my old street in Greenwich, I saw people in dressing gowns had gathered out of their beds to witness the spectacle. I got out of the car as I watched my house – or what was left of it. A bare skeleton now, the flames had eaten their way through it. I watched, dismayed and confused about how this could have happened. There were fire engines, an ambulance, and police cars with their lights flashing red and blue. A police officer stood by the crowd to keep everything under control. I made my way to the pavement with my heart in my mouth. A policewoman turned to me.

'Stay back, madam,' she said.

'But – that is my house,' I said, pointing at what was left of it.

'You live there?'

'No, I was trying to sell it. I live elsewhere.'

'Please stay here,' she said.

A swarm of firefighters came out, the sky was thick with smoke and the acrid odour of the fire could be smelt everywhere in the air and on my clothes. The police officer told me to wait inside a marked car. Another policeman came forward and asked me more questions. *Was this my house? Where did I live if this house was for sale? Why was it for sale?* He went away, and there was another long wait. It was morning then, and the crowd had eased. I made out Mrs. Parker and Olivia. Of course, Mrs. Parker would stand by and watch the excitement. They saw me sitting in the back of a police car, and there was something on their faces I couldn't quite read.

Another police officer came and told me they would take me to the station to ask me more questions and take my statement, but they didn't tell me what had caused the fire. They asked question after question, but if I asked one in return, it went unanswered. My mind raced. Did I need a lawyer? But for what? I had done nothing wrong. Someone did this, though. The person who sent the roses and attacked Sasha and Anna – I was sure of it. That person had set fire to my house to make sure I had nothing to sell. To make a statement. But who was doing this? Who had I pissed off that much to go to such lengths? My mind swirled, and I went back to the moment when I realised Lucien wasn't in bed with me. He wouldn't set fire to my house, would he? I had to stop with this suspicion of him somehow being connected to this. But why did he leave? Where did he go? He didn't call or send a text to explain his departure.

At the police station, I was told to wait in a room with grey walls and metal chairs. There were posters on the walls about the dangers of drunk driving. There should be another poster of what a hazard people were in general. My hands trembled, and my knees twitched with nerves. A female detective walked in. Her dark hair was swept back with a simple ponytail, and she wore a grey suit, a white skirt, and flat, sensible shoes. I couldn't help but think how clean she looked. A simple outfit, yet so effortless. She introduced herself as DC Alison Norris. She asked me the same questions the other police officers had asked.

'Can you think of anyone who might do this?' she asked.

If there was an electricity fault, she wouldn't ask me that question, would she? She had to suspect that the fire was deliberate. I had no choice but to tell her about everything: the roses, the attacks on Anna and Sasha. It seemed to go on and on. I finally told her to check with Ben Miller, as I had already told him all of this.

'How do you know DC Miller?' she asked.

'He investigated the previous case of Amelia and Henry Jones.'

She raised an eyebrow at me, thinking I was a woman who got herself involved in a lot of sticky situations.

'Your house has its history, doesn't it?' she asked.

'A married couple used to live there before, and the wife went missing,' I explained.

'And someone wanted it destroyed.'

She left shortly after that declaration, which left a thick cloud hanging in the room as I waited once more. Hours passed, and I thought I would remain there forever with a trail of detectives asking me questions. My fingers trembled, and I would have given anything to have a drop of wine. Then, finally, the door opened after what seemed a lifetime and Alison appeared again, followed by Ben. I swallowed, and my hands clutched into fists as anger rose like acid. So, this was his new partner. Quite an upgrade from Sparks. His eyes passed through me, but there was no anger. If there was someone who should be angry, it was me. He had no right to that anger. He sat beside Alison, and I avoided looking at him while she went on with asking questions – some new, some the same.

'You were having trouble selling that house, weren't you?' Alison asked.

I didn't like the direction this interview was heading. She made it sound like I stomped into the house with a can of gasoline and a box of matches in my pocket and torched it to flames. Then, when Ben spoke, his voice made me jump.

'The house was insured, wasn't it?' he asked.

The question expanded in the room. *What was this? Did he think I—?*

'Yes, it was.'

'Where were you last night, Ms. Clarke?' he asked.

We were back on a last-name basis again, as if he hadn't been in my bed and hid the fact he was married, making me look like a tit. The door opened, and a uniformed policeman appeared. Alison stood, and Ben looked at me as if to say he was sorry. I looked away as he stood and followed Alison out. Then there was another long wait, and all I wanted was a decent cup of coffee – which I wasn't getting from there – and to go pee.

The door opened once more, and I sat up straight. Alison told me I was free to go, but she handed me her card on the way out. Lucien and Olivia stood in the corridor. Lucien came to me and put his arms around me while Olivia patted my shoulders.

'Let's get you out of here,' Lucien said, and he led the way.

I glanced over my shoulder to where Ben stood, watching us, and there was a look on his face that I couldn't quite read.

Chapter Forty-four

Lucien had heard about what happened at the house and was looking for me. Olivia told him she saw me in the back of a police car, being escorted to the police station. The police had also asked him a few questions, and he vouched for me that I was at home because he was with me. I wondered what Ben thought about that, but I truly didn't care. He was the one who lied about being married, not Lucien. At least, despite his flaws, Lucien was open about who he was and the people he saw, and he was shameless about it. He took me back home, where Olivia made tea and Lucien made me go to bed and rest.

'What caused the fire?' I asked, after he helped me out of my jacket.

'Don't think about that now. Get some rest,' he said tenderly.

'Where were you?' I asked. 'You weren't in bed?'

'I went for a walk.'

'In the dead of night?'

'It was five o'clock in the morning,' he reasoned.

'Do you go for walks early in the morning a lot?'

'When I can't sleep, yes.'

'Can you lie down with me?' I asked.

'Of course, Emily,' he said.

Despite how shitty things were, I slept like the dead. When I woke, it was light out. Had I slept throughout the day and night?

I got up from the bed, and Lucien wasn't there. I called for him, but no answer came. I went to the bathroom, brushed my teeth, and cried in the shower for the mess my life was. For how unhappy I was. I stayed there until the water turned cold, then I got dressed and called for Lucien again, even though I knew there was no point. He wasn't there. Where did he go? Where was my phone? I went to the bedroom and looked for it on the bedside table. It wasn't there. I searched under the duvet and pillows. Nothing. I knelt on the floor on all fours and checked under the bed. There was dust, but no phone. It had to be in the jacket. Where was the jacket? My memory was hazy, and I wasn't sure what had happened after Lucien and Olivia took me home. I remembered Lucien escorting me to the bedroom after Olivia had made me a cup of tea, and then him lying next to me. Lucien had helped me out of my jacket in the bedroom. So where was it? I decided not to bother with retracing my steps. The phone was the least of my worries anyway. I shuffled out of the bedroom and stopped dead. With his feet propped up on my desk, sat Travis. My laptop and diary were on the floor next to the desk. I blinked at him in disbelief. *How did he get in? Did Lucien let him in the house to watch out for me? Why would he do that? To run an errand?* Travis's long fringe was swept aside, exposing his sweet, exquisite face. He surveyed me carefully, then his lips curled into a snarl and my body went cold. Lucien didn't let him in. He came in uninvited. Next to my laptop and diary was my phone, lying face down. How long had he been here?

'How did you get in?' I asked.

'Sit down, Emily. It's about time you and I had a chat, don't you agree?'

I disagreed, but I sat down on the chair anyway. 'I thought we did when you stalked me to the coffee shop?'

He narrowed his eyes. 'And you didn't listen.'

I rubbed my face with my hands. 'You broke into my house because of this?'

'Why can't you just stay away?' he asked.

'I don't have time for this… You should discuss this with Lucien, not me.'

Travis smiled. 'Lucien sets all the rules and changes them when it suits him.'

'What does this have to do with me?' I asked.

'This has everything to do with you. You are what he wants. Not me, Jan, Sasha or Cassie.'

'Who is Cassie?' I asked.

'The redhead who can't keep her filthy hands off him.'

'Oh,' I said.

'He was so angry after what happened with his parents. He blamed you and vowed he would never speak to you again. Then one day, I caught him peeking through your Facebook and the chat box was open. He was trying to get in touch with you.'

'When was this?' I asked.

'When you posted a picture of yourself with your parents on the boat.'

It started to come together. Travis didn't speak to me when we were at the club, and I paid no attention to it. Why should I care if a twenty-something with pink hair came and introduced himself or not? Then he argued with Lucien that night and stormed off. Lucien had told me he broke things off with Travis. Lucien had seen the photo I posted on Facebook. Of course, he did. He might have been angry at the time, but he didn't remove me from his friend list, just as I didn't. He was watching me as I was watching him, but he wasn't the only one watching. Travis was too. Travis couldn't see my profile unless I had him as a friend, but I didn't have to work hard to know what he did. He might have taken Lucien's phone or gone through his laptop and looked me up from Lucien's profile. What had Lucien said about Travis? That he was possessive. So much so that he wanted Lucien all to himself. Sasha had pointed this out too. Then there was the other night when I went to the apartment, how Lucien was annoyed and somewhat uncomfortable when Travis knocked on the door demanding to be let in. Lucien had found someone that was like his mother. That meant – oh, dear God. I stared at him with my mouth gaped open, fish-like.

'It was you,' I said. 'You sent me the roses.'

'Finally, we're getting somewhere,' he said.

'And you placed roses in the apartment you share with Lucien for him to find. Why?'

'The Baccara rose is quite beautiful, isn't it?'

'It is, yes, but why? Roses are associated with romance, not hate.'

He stood from the chair. 'It's a statement.'

'A statement?' I asked, confused.

He leaned against my desk. 'You don't have to know the reason behind the madness. I knew it would work since I managed to freak both of you out. Lucien didn't take it seriously. First, he thought it was a secret admirer and left the rose on the counter to wilt. I understood then how he felt about us.'

'Why don't you just call it a day instead of doing this? You're so young.'

He glared at me. 'Because I love him. I have to watch him go back and forth with other people. It's humiliating.'

'He told me you had an open relationship.'

'That's what he likes to believe.'

I glanced down at the floor, and there was a red-wine stain that seemed to have penetrated there. Another thing came to me like a foot kicking my stomach. The attacks on Anna and Sasha were done by him too?

My head shot up in his direction. 'Was it you? The one who attacked Anna and Sasha?'

Travis swept his perfect fringe off his face, saying nothing yet indicating that he did. Sweet Jesus.

'And my house catching fire, was it you? That was the last straw, wasn't it? You saw me at the apartment, and you knew he snuck out to come here. So, you followed him.'

'I knew you two had fucked. Why would he spend the night if it didn't benefit him? He's selfish like that.'

'He's not selfish.'

'Yes, he is just like his bitch of a mother. But do you honestly believe that she turned out that way just because of what had happened with his brother? Do you? The experience didn't help, but he didn't make life easy for her.'

'What are you talking about?' I asked. 'She was obsessed with him and wanted to keep him to herself just like you! So why go after my friend and Sasha? What have they done to you?'

'I wanted to hurt you both.'

'We went through something nobody could understand. Why attack innocent people?'

'Because they are important to you both.'

'You're insane.'

'Wrong, Emily, you have to be sane to pull off what I did and not be caught.'

'Listen to me,' I pleaded. 'You're still young. It's not too late.'

'It is too late now,' he said.

Chapter Forty-five

What did he mean by 'too late'? Too late for what? What was he going to do? Where was Lucien? I scanned around the room, trying to look for something, anything. Suddenly I was back in my old house, where Amelia had made her way into it. Like her, Travis didn't seem to be armed, and he was too skinny and frail-looking to overpower me, but he had attacked Anna and Sasha and inflicted pain on their bodies. I shouldn't let his appearance fool me. I had to somehow keep him talking while trying to manoeuvre some sort of a plan. Maybe Lucien would come back, and then what? There was a large possibility that Travis would hurt him. I couldn't bear for another person to get hurt. Why couldn't Lucien be clear about his feelings and be upfront? Why was Lucien looking at my profile while I had to be like the others and post that stupid photo on Facebook for the world to see? Travis peered at me as if trying to identify something. Jealousy made people do a lot of foolish things, same with love.

'I never liked you,' Travis said.

I said nothing to that.

'The moment I saw you in that club wearing that awful, ridiculous dress and pretending to be someone you're not, craving his attention. It was pathetic. Lucien, of course, was used to it. You're ten years older than him, so surely you could find someone your own age. You're not a bad-looking woman. We argued that night about you. I knew what his intentions were inviting you to that club. He planned to fuck you that night, which I know he did.'

'How?' I asked.

'He told me.'

I rose an eyebrow. 'Lucien told you?'

'I asked him, and he told me. He described your… escapades as… lovely. But, of course, you're not the best he has ever had, despite being older than him.'

My anger flared. Did Lucien tell him this when they were in bed? Why did he have to blabber what happened between us? Why couldn't he just keep it to himself? Was he trying to show off? To look cool? Some things were meant to be kept private. If Travis was even saying the truth. He could be lying for all I knew, but how he could have known what happened in the club when he left? Lucien did tell him, and I was hurt that he did. It was stupid of him, knowing the kind of person Travis was.

'We talked about everything,' Travis went on. 'And, sex with him was incredible. Cassie was his best fuck,' Travis said.

Did Lucien actually tell him that the best sex he ever had was with Cassie? That image came to me of the redhead straddling him, how intimate the gesture was. Then the image faded to something more sensual and grotesque – her naked and moaning, her eyes closed with the feverish ecstasy. Tiny sparks ignited in me. It was irresponsible of Lucien to drop names like that to a boyfriend who was so possessive. A little jealousy was healthy in every relationship, but he should have known better and realised Travis's jealousy even extended to the extremes. Sex was another dangerous hazard, and all of this was about that. Cassie could be next, yet Travis was here because Lucien didn't love Cassie. He loved me. What was this love he had for me? He was out of my league, and I wasn't just older than him, but ancient.

'He's just so beautiful,' Travis said. 'So flawed at the same time.'

'What is your plan, Travis? Are you going to kill me?'

His expression was unreadable. 'No.'

What he was going to do? Beat me? I had to keep him talking.

'The roses,' I asked. 'Where did you get them?'

'My mother grows them. She's a florist, but she doesn't sell them in her store.'

That made sense. Though why didn't she sell them? I thought of that afternoon when I snuck into Olivia's backyard to see if she had grown those particular roses. How silly I had been to suspect her when she had been protecting Lucien all along. Lucien was just a name for some, but it meant light, elegance and ethereal, which couldn't be more suited for the man who owned it. He wore that name with pride. This name to me meant so many things: the name of my old neighbour, a friend and a lover. Now, it manifested into chaos. Despair. It was beautiful, but it came with a price. Didn't Lucien suspect that with Travis's mum being a florist, the roses might have come from her garden? But did we ever suspect the ones closest to us? Yet the ones closest to us were the ones who were likely to cause us harm. The ones that knew us best, our habits and routines.

'Why not?' I asked

He sighed as if my questions bored him. 'It really doesn't matter.'

'Were you the one who put grease on the bathroom floor and took my wallet?'

'Enough with the questions.'

'You said we needed to chat. I'm only obeying this request.'

'Yes, it was me.'

'How—'

'I knew you had the camera, but only by the front door. You need to upgrade your security, Emily. As for the wallet, you're clumsy, and the drinking doesn't help. That's what he turned you into, a drunk.'

'I'm not—'

'I saw you,' he interrupted, 'at the pub talking to Jan. You like him, don't you?'

'Well… he's quite lovely to look at.'

'Of course, but you want him, don't you, Emily? But you're too proper, and you wouldn't do that to Lucien.'

'Do what?'

'Fuck his best mate.'

'I don't want to sleep with him.'

'What about Anna?'

'What about her?'

'Do you honestly believe she didn't sleep with him?' he asked.

'I really don't care about my friend's sex life. She's a grown woman, and she can sleep with whomever she likes.'

A sound came from outside: a car rumbling by, and then a shout. Travis hadn't averted his eyes from me. People were out there going about their lives while I was there, isolated, as if I wasn't part of that world. People got murdered while others focused on their routines. If I screamed, what would he do? Screaming was enough to disrupt people from their tasks. Another sound came from outside. Voices this time, from the neighbours next door. Travis wasn't standing far enough for me to rush to the door. He would be able to keep up with me. He said he had no intention of killing me, so what did he want?

'What do you want me to do? Stay out of the way? I will do that if that's what you want, but that won't change Lucien's ways….' I was going to say that Lucien had already dumped him twice, but making Travis angry wasn't wise.

'You should have stayed away when I told you to.'

'But—'

The front door opened, and Travis looked up, his hand reaching for something on his back. What did he have there? A knife? A gun? I shut my eyes, not wishing to witness what was going to happen.

'Travis? W-w-what are you doing here?'

It was Lucien. *Dear God, don't let anything happen to him.* How could he be so careless, after knowing what I had been going through, what he was going through, to leave without locking the front door? Where did he go? What was so important that he had to leave? Travis must have been watching the house, waiting for Lucien to go.

Chapter Forty-six

Travis and Lucien stared at each other while I remained glued to the sofa. Lucien was holding a brown shopping bag. He turned to me, and for a horrible second, I thought they were in it together until I saw the dread in his eyes as if, deep down, he knew this was coming but didn't truly expect this type of outcome. The realisation sank in what this all meant. This was about him. It was Travis all along.

'Are you all right?' he asked.

I nodded.

His eyes swept away from me and landed back on his ex-lover. 'What is this about?'

There was an authority in his voice I had never heard before.

'You know what is this about,' Travis spat.

'Leave her out of this,' Lucien said.

'Give me your phone,' Travis demanded.

'What?'

'Give me the fucking phone!' Travis ordered.

Lucien slipped his hand in the back of his black jeans, took out his phone and handed it to Travis. Travis took the phone and threw it on the floor next to my laptop and phone.

'Sit down, Lucien!' Travis shouted.

Lucien glared back at him and took a seat on the armchair.

'I had to watch you go from one person to another,' Travis said more calmly, 'without any disregard for my feelings.'

Lucien's dark eyebrow rose. 'Your feelings? We have been through this!'

Losing his temper wasn't going to get us anywhere but killed, so he had better ease with the attitude, especially when Travis had the upper hand.

'For fuck's sake,' Lucien went on. 'After what my parents put me through, this is the last thing I need.'

This wasn't the time to whine either. I glanced at the lamp next to me. I could launch it at Travis, but he could be armed. Did he take one of my knives from the block in the kitchen? I couldn't see from where I sat. My heart raced with trepidation, and sweat broke out on my back.

'So, all of it, it was you?' Lucien asked.

'What do you think?'

'Why?'

'Why don't you love me?' Travis asked.

'I do love you,' Lucien said.

Travis pointed his finger at me. 'But you love her too?'

Lucien glanced at me as if he was aware of me for the first time. He cast me a sad look as if to say, *Forgive me for what I'm about to say*. I was beyond caring what he would say at that point. I wanted this to be over.

'Well, she's a nice lay,' Lucien said.

'Everything is about sex with you,' Travis said.

'Travis, let Emily go, and we will talk about this,' Lucien reasoned.

'No,' Travis said.

Lucien ran his fingers through his hair in frustration. 'I'm messed up, okay? So why go after Sasha?'

'Because you fucked her!' Travis snarled.

'That was way before I knew you existed, you knob head,' Lucien spat.

'You're like a dog with two dicks, you know that?' Travis said savagely.

'Boys, please,' I said.

They cast a murderous look at each other as Travis leaned back on the desk and the silence prickled between us. While I tried to think of a way out, Lucien inspected the rings on his fingers and Travis was contemplating something. There were two of us, one of him. We could overpower him.

'What are you going to do? Keep us here as hostages?' Lucien asked. 'Jan is going to know something is up.'

'Jan can go fuck himself,' Travis said.

'After what he did for you,' Lucien said. 'You're so ungrateful. It's an issue I have with you.'

'And you're selfish,' Travis said.

'How am I selfish?' Lucien asked, his voice full of contempt. 'I was upfront with you from the start. You're the one who wouldn't listen. I never promised you anything.'

'Tell me, Lucien, would you start a relationship with her if you had a chance?'

Lucien looked at me with dispassion. 'No.'

'*Liar*!' Travis exclaimed. 'Such bullshit.'

'Believe what you will,' Lucien said in a bored tone.

'She's a naughty minx. She slept with a married man.'

I raised my head at this.

'She didn't know he was married,' Lucien said.

'That was you too? You sent the photos to his wife?' I asked.

'It was pretty hilarious,' Travis said.

'You little *shit*!' I exclaimed.

'What are you going to do with us? You know how this is going to end, right?' Lucien asked.

'So confident, aren't you?' Travis said.

'Come on, Travis, you don't have to do this,' Lucien argued.

Tears smeared down Travis's cheeks. 'It's too late for that now.'

'It's not too late,' Lucien said. 'There is always a way.'

'No, I have gone too far,' Travis said.

I glanced over at Lucien, and he shook his head at me, then the front door burst open and swung to the wall. It all happened so quickly I could hardly process the commotion. Travis took something out of his back – a gun. Lucien had risen to his feet. I, too, stood as Ben stood by the door, aiming his gun. He said something, but I wasn't sure what. Travis wasn't aiming the gun at Lucien, but rather at me. Ben was reasoning with Travis not to do this, telling him it wasn't worth it. Lucien had taken a step forward, and Ben warned him not to move either. Fear gripped my insides, twisting them like an iron fist as shots were fired.

Chapter Forty-seven

My ears were still ringing from the gunshots as I sat in the waiting room at the hospital, where time seemed to have slowed. Ben had eventually figured it out, it was Travis all along. He didn't get into the specifics of how he knew, not yet at least. There hadn't been much time, not with all the events unfolding in my house. Travis had broken so many laws, and his future wasn't looking bright. What a waste. Ben had shot him in the leg, enough to bring him down, but as Lucien stepped towards him, Travis turned his aim at him and shot Lucien in the stomach. He was in surgery now. My clothes were covered with his blood. After Lucien was shot, I went to him and tried to help him, and Ben urged me to put pressure on the wound while he called for backup. What a disaster. And for what? I spent hours drinking black coffee from the vending machine in that waiting room. There was a man I didn't know in the waiting room, and I saw a packet of cigarettes peeking through his jeans.

'May I have one?' I asked.

He looked at me as if I had awakened him from a nightmare. Was his story just as bad as mine? *We all had our crosses to bear.*

'A cigarette?' I said, pointing my finger at the packet.

'Oh,' he said. 'Sure.'

I noticed his skin was dark, his hair black and short, and his face had intricate features. He took a cigarette and handed it to me along with a lighter. I stood, went outside the hospital, and smoked. I wasn't one to smoke usually, but today I needed it.

When I returned to the waiting room, Jan had arrived and walked up to me, his face contoured with anger and distress. He grabbed me by the shoulder, his eyes frantic.

'What the fuck happened?' he demanded.

'You probably need to sit down,' I said.

And so, he sat and crossed his elegant legs as I started from the beginning. After I finished, his face was as white as a sheet, and tears smeared down his cheeks.

'I can't believe that wispy fucker shot him,' he said.

Jan urged me to go home, but how could I go home when it was a crime scene? Another house of mine was tainted by a tragedy. How many houses were going to turn into shit because I stepped inside them?

#

He was lucky, I had been told. If the bullet went through an inch higher, it would have killed him. Did Lucien see himself as lucky? I walked along the white corridors, and the antiseptic smell was thick in the air. It was raining out, and my hair was wet from the rain. I located Lucien's room, but I didn't go in right away. There were lots of flowers in the room, along with balloons and cards. Lucien was propped up on the pillows with an IV needle attached to his arm, there were dark circles under his eyes, and he was looking at something in front of him on the table. Olivia was sitting on the armchair, holding his hand. On the table was a wooden box, and it looked like it was made from oak. Olivia patted his hand and stood. I moved away. I didn't want to speak to her; I would later, but not at that instant. I hurried away before she spotted me, and I slipped into the bathroom.

In the bathroom, I took a small bottle of vodka from my bag, then looked down at the bottle. Enough of this. A guy took a bullet for me; I had to stop this. I poured the bottle down the sink, waited five minutes, and then came out again.

I approached the room, and Lucien was alone and staring at the opened box. He looked so young, so innocent and so, so sad. Like me, he was unhappy trying to find his place after the events that happened last year. He looked away from the box towards the window, and with one hand, he weakly moved the box away until it reached the edge and dropped to the floor. It made a loud thud as something silvery slipped out of it onto the floor. The two pedants he and Sylvian had worn. Who had bought them? Olivia? Jan? I tapped on the door and walked towards the box, and as I attempted to pick it up, he shook his head and glanced towards the window. I went to the bed and ran my hand on his white hair – so beautiful.

'It will be all right,' I assured him.

An overpowering sense of love and tenderness engulfed me.

He turned his head in my direction and took my hand. 'I'm going to be good. I don't want to fuck around any more… it's not the life I want to live.'

I smiled at him and squeezed his hand. 'Don't think about that now.'

'No,' he argued and winced. 'That night when Anna was attacked, he told me he was going out… and before he left… he looked at me so strangely. That was why I asked for the dates, but I couldn't believe…'

'Shhh…'

'I was so stupid… I shouldn't have told him… about you… us… but I had no idea that it would trigger him like that. I want to be a better person.' He coughed. 'I'm going to be better.'

I ran my hand through his hair that spread on the pillow. 'And you will.'

Chapter Forty-eight

The prison looked exactly as I imagined: grim, dark and forbidding. Two squat stone towers stood on either side of a vast wooden door.

There was already a knot of people by the entrance, mostly women, dressed for the cold. The older women were in thick coats, woolly hats and boots, and younger women were in sweatpants, their hair piled up on their heads, eyes heavy with mascara. There was a hardness about their expressions. No one was there for fun. One or two glanced at me as I joined them, registering the fact I was a new face, that I was different from most of them – a bit better educated, more advantaged. I kept my head down, kept my distance and waited.

A guard unlocked the side door and checked off names on a clipboard list as the women pressed forward.

Inside the prison, the officers pointed me inside and walked me through the procedures, recognising I was new.

The chairs were plain, institutional, with curved metal backs and seats. I gripped the cool metal arms and tried not to look at the other women who were speaking in low voices.

An officer did the rounds, matching our IDs to our pinched faces. He did a second name check, and my heart thudded. They beckoned us to move forward, and we filed in one by one.

Finally, a female officer patted me down, checking to be sure I wasn't concealing anything that I shouldn't take in.

The visiting room loomed ahead and we queued up at the entrance. From the little I could see, peering around the women ahead of me, it reminded me of an airport lounge.

The guard checked me off yet another list, then nodded me in.

'Table twenty. On the right.'

For a moment, I was afraid to move. I looked around and I saw him. His gaze hit mine, then fell to his hands, resting lightly on the edge of the table. His jaw was hard.

I thought I was prepared, but I wasn't. For a second, I felt disorientated, almost dizzy, and I couldn't speak. I managed to pull out the chair opposite his, and sat down.

'Hello,' I said stupidly.

He shifted his weight and sat back in his seat, with one leg crossed at the knee. His cheeks were hollowed. Lack of sleep, perhaps. Or poor food.

Finally, without looking at me, he said quietly, 'You shouldn't have come.'

Guards stood along the walls, scanning us all, watching.

I sat forward and lowered my voice, willed him to move closer.

'Henry, I needed to see you. I don't know if you heard, but something awful happened….'

He kept his eyes low. His face was closed-off and sad.

'It's Lucien. He's…' I felt my eyes water, but I willed myself to go on, 'He has been shot.'

Henry didn't move.

I said, as calmly as I could, 'It was this guy he was dating… Travis. He became fixated on Lucien. He started to send flowers to him and me. Then he attacked my friend and Sasha… and finally he came to my house… and….'

After a long pause, when I was unable to go on, Henry responded.

'This is what happens when a man lacks moral code. He mixes himself with bad people. I never agreed with his lifestyle.' He lifted a hand and raked it through his hair.

I lowered my head. I didn't know why I came all the way here. To try to fix a relationship between a father and son that couldn't be repaired? To make Henry understand? Because although Henry was not Lucien's father by blood, he surely had the right to know.

'Amelia, she let him do whatever he wanted, and now look how he turned out,' Henry said.

'And how do you think he turned out?' I asked.

'Looking like a girl, modelling, taking photographs, dating men and women… it's not natural….'

Says who? I thought. But I wasn't going to get into that with Henry. He was a man of certain principles. A man's man.

'How come you two are still speaking?' Henry asked with genuine curiosity.

'We reconnected. He told me you want nothing to do with him. Why is that?'

Henry broke eye contact. 'Guilt.'

'Guilt?'

'For the way I treated that boy… He didn't deserve any of that.'

'But why do you refuse to have anything to do with him? He's so broken about that… He keeps wondering why you don't love him.'

Henry looked up. 'Is that what he thinks? That I don't love him?'

'Yes,' I replied.

'That's where he's very wrong. I love that boy with all of my might. I tried to protect him from his mother. I knew what she was like. I didn't agree with his lifestyle and the promiscuity. As I said, Amelia let him to do whatever he wanted. I knew what she was doing. I'm not saying she's a bad mother, but after Sylvian's accident, it drove a wedge between us. This was a woman I promised to spend my life with.'

He lowered his head and inspected his hands. The very hands that had shoved his own flesh and blood down a well.

'I couldn't believe she would even suggest… that we… well, you know the outcome.'

'But why didn't you go behind her back and report it?' I asked.

Henry shook his head as if this was a lost cause. 'She would have killed me. You have no idea what it was like.'

'But why yell at Lucien? I saw you shove him and verbally abuse him.'

'I'm not saying what I did was right. I knew he wasn't mine. A father knows those things. You have to understand the kind of woman I married.'

'But didn't you see the signs before you married her?'

Henry eyed me. 'Did you see the signs?'

'Well, I did think she was… odd… but I thought the disappearance of Sylvian made her that way.'

'No, that was karma for all the horrible things she had done. You can't keep something like that hidden and expect not to lose your mind. When I met Amelia… I was so star-struck by her beauty. Lucien looks so much like her it killed me.'

'How did you two meet? If you don't mind me asking.'

'I used to walk by that bakery, and one day, I saw this girl with white-blonde hair opening the store, and all I could do was stop and stare. She was the most beautiful woman I had ever seen.'

I recalled the pictures I had seen of her when she was younger – before, as Henry said, karma started to eat at her – and yes, she was so stunning she could have been a model or an actress. She possessed the kind of beauty that made you want to weep.

'But I had no idea how rotten she was,' Henry went on.

'When did you start to notice disturbing behaviour?'

'When Lucien was born, she threatened my career that if I left her, she would say that I hit her and she would poison me… Those kind of things. Things like that wouldn't be taken lightly in the army. What was I supposed to do? I was trapped. I couldn't believe she cheated on me.'

'But you cheated on her too,' I pointed out.

'Can you imagine waking up to a living hell every single day? That couple moved in, and the wife was always friendly with me, too friendly. Amelia and I might have slept in the same bed, but she wouldn't let me touch her. I'm human. Lucien was fully aware of the state of our marriage.'

'Why did you confess to her about the affair knowing what she was capable of?'

Henry looked up at the ceiling. 'Honour.'

And a woman was killed because of his honour.

'I had no idea she would—' Henry said, then paused abruptly.

'Did you suspect Amelia had something to do with Amanda's disappearance?'

'No, I honestly had no idea she would go after her. How she pulled it off was beyond me, as was what she did to your ex.'

I lowered my head.

'How is he? How is Lucien?' Henry asked.

'He has been released from surgery, but he will remain in hospital for the time being under superv—'

Henry broke down and fat tears rolled down on his cheeks. 'Poor boy. That poor boy.'

I lowered my eyes in sadness. 'Yes.'

Henry wiped the tears from his eyes with his fingers. 'Can you do me a favour?'

The man had tried to warn me against his wife, but I wasn't sure if I owed him any favours.

'Can you take care of him for me?'

'Lucien is stronger than you think. He is more than capable.'

'I know he's a tough one, but you're something else to him.'

'How do you know?'

'I know.'

The guard was making his rounds, breaking up the couples, calling time. *I was something else to him.*

'Tell him to come and see me when he recovers. I want to see him.'

I had to find a way to break this to Lucien, as I wasn't planning to tell him that I went to prison to visit Henry. I'd wait until after Lucien had been released; I couldn't throw this at him whilst he was lying in a hospital bed. The gory image came to me once more – when he was shot and bleeding out. I thought he was going to die because he lost so much blood.

I nodded as Henry stood from the chair and watched as the guards ordered them into line and counted them off the list. Finally, the door opened and they shuffled through, swallowed into the body of the prison.

I left the prison and took a taxi to the hospital to visit Lucien. I watched the passing streets with people going about their day, running errands, going to work or going to the supermarket to stock their cupboards with food, and a thought came to me then. Really beautiful people do attract a lot of sorrow.

#

Secrets and Lies J.S. Ellis

The Secret They Kept: Book 1

Emily Clarke thought her dreams were coming true. Her business was thriving and she was moving into a beautiful new house. Yet this dream quickly morphed into a nightmare.

Rocks being thrown at her windows. Haunting messages written on glass. Items mysteriously disappearing.

Emily's nerves are on edge, which is only made worse by the man across the street constantly screaming at his wife. By befriending their son, Lucien, she learns a dark truth about the street she now calls home. Lucien has a brother who went missing ten years ago, as did the last occupant of Emily's house.

Emily wants to believe these ominous events are past history until her ex-boyfriend vanishes without a trace. Now, she's convinced she is a pawn in someone's twisted game.

Can she uncover who is behind these disappearances before becoming their next victim?

The Secret She Kept

 Days before her murder, Anthony's friend Lottie lent him her laptop. Curiosity getting the best of him, he clicks on a file and finds videos recorded by her in the year leading up to her death. Within those recordings, she exposes dark secrets someone will kill to keep hidden, and Lottie's toxic relationship with Anthony's long-time friend, Davian.

When Anthony's childhood friend, Davian, is placed under arrest for the murder, Anthony refuses to believe he could do such a thing, but Lottie was infatuated by Davian. More damning evidence piles up. Anthony wonders if it's possible a man he's known for most of his life has kept a sinister side of himself hidden.

Now, Anthony faces an impossible choice; turn the laptop over to the police and risk being accused of hindering the investigation, or try to solve the case himself. Lottie gave him the computer for a reason. There was something there she wanted him to see. Can he put the pieces of the puzzle together in time to uncover the killer?

In Her Words

While she seems to have it all, Sophie Knight is looking for more. When gorgeous and carefree Michael Frisk walks into her life, he offers the excitement and passion she desires.

Sophie is willing to risk everything she has. After all, she is used to concealing things from her husband—like her alcoholism, her unhappiness. But soon she has more to hide. She wakes up one morning in an alcoholic haze and finds bruises on her body, but has no recollection of what happened to her. Was she raped?

When unsettling notes and mysterious phone calls start, Sophie wonders whom she should turn to. Is Michael the cause of the frightening things happening in her life, or is he the answer to her problems?

Theodore: The neighbour's Cat

My roommate is a serial killer.

And I have been powerless to stop him because I... am a cat.

Don't get me wrong, Dean has never been cruel to me. He provides me with shelter, toys, and plenty of affection. But I have seen his dark side, his brutal treatment of women, and I can't bear to watch anyone else get hurt.

Jane from next door is attractive for a human, not to mention being incredibly kind. That kindness may get her killed. I've seen how Dean looks at her, I know what he's plotting. In his mind, she's his for the taking. I wasn't able to save the others, but I'm not ready to give up. One way or another, I have to figure out how to communicate to Jane that she's in danger.

Can I find a way to warn her in time? Or will she become just another name on his growing list of victims?

Secrets and Lies J.S. Ellis

The Rich Man

Her beloved disappeared without a word.

When a web of deceit tightens, can a young woman uncover the truth before she's the next to get ghosted? Elena Gomez's heart aches over her boyfriend's betrayal. But determined to pick up the pieces, she squares her shoulders and struggles to rebuild.

And when a handsome and wealthy widower sweeps into her life, she dares hope he's the answer to her prayers. Blossoming under his devoted attention, Elena soon finds herself falling hard for his magnetic charm.

But when she discovers the odd events surrounding his late wife's death, a series of unnerving coincidences send her pulse racing with dread. And when a ghost from her past returns, she fears she's stepped into a trap that could cost her everything.

Can she escape the darkness closing in, or will she be pulled six feet under?

Lost and Found: Book 1

 Despite being polar opposites, Phoebe and Adele's friendship has stretched on for years. One a bubbly blonde, the other raven-haired and studious. They seem to have nothing in common, yet the bond between them is unbreakable.

Or so Phoebe thought.

She never believed Adele would hide anything from her until she sees her sneaking off with her handsome neighbour. Feeling betrayed, Phoebe begins to see cracks in their friendship she never noticed before.

Then, Adele vanishes.

Fearing for Adele's safety, Phoebe searches for clues about her disappearance. However, the deeper she digs, the more she realizes she didn't know Adele as well as she thought. Yet as revelations come to light, one mystery remains. What happened to Adele? And how is her disappearance connected to the stranger next door?

Secrets and Lies J.S. Ellis

Hide and Seek: Book 2

Hope is waning with Phoebe no closer to finding her best friend, Adele. Her suspicions involving her neighbour, Alan, have been cleared, leaving her no other hunches to pursue.

Until the letter arrives.

A message, written in Adele's hand, paints a picture of a side of her friend's life Phoebe never knew. Renewed with the optimism that she is still alive, Phoebe launches back into the investigation. Among the pages of Adele's communications, Phoebe finds evidence pointing to an unlikely suspect...

And yet another connection to Alan.

He seemed so concerned about the investigation, wanting to help in any way he could. Was the man next door a genuine ally? Or working to protect the real culprit?

The Confidant

Secrets have deadly consequences.

A part of him knew she was always lying, but he could change that. He could change her.

When charismatic Zoë first sits in Jason's salon chair, he can immediately tell they have a connection. Who wouldn't? She was smart, witty, and incredibly funny, everything someone could want in a budding friendship. But soon, Jason learns there is more to Zoë than meets the eye.

When lies are uncovered and secrets exposed, Jason must decide just how far he's willing to go in the name of friendship.

How far should he go to uncover the truth? If he digs too deep, could Jason lose the very person he's trying to keep?

When it all comes crashing to the light, and someone's very life hangs in the balance, will he regret what he's done? Or will Jason wish he had only done more?

Secrets and Lies J.S. Ellis

Till Death Do Us Part.

Abigail thought she achieved the ultimate fairy tale. Handsome movie star meets small-island hotel employee and sweeps her away to his glorious Hollywood mansion. Everything about Carson Levin seems too good to be true… until she steps inside his home.

Every inch of it is just as his sex symbol wife, Taira Anderson, left it before her fatal car accident. But the oddities don't end there.

A presence wanders the halls.

High heels clicking over the floor.

Mysterious splashes in the pool.

The bath filling with water without a soul in sight.

Something or someone is trying to send Abigail a message. But is it a warning… or a threat?

Scan the code to purchase.

Note from The Author

If you enjoy what I write, you can help this little writer out by writing a review on Amazon or Goodreads or any platform of your choice. Reviews are the lifeline for authors and readers trust other readers. If you use social media, spread the word. It will be wonderful to have my book listed with others you have enjoyed.

You can leave a review

Love,

J.S Ellis xx

You can sign up for my newsletter and keep updated with new releases, offers, updates and giveaways.

Secrets and Lies J.S. Ellis

https://joannewritesbooks.com

Note from The Author

If you enjoy what I write, you can help this little writer out by writing a review on Amazon or Goodreads or any platform of your choice. Reviews are the lifeline for authors and readers trust other readers. If you use social media, spread the word. It will be wonderful to have my book listed with others you have enjoyed.

Love,

J.S Ellis xx

You can sign up for my newsletter and keep updated with new releases, offers, updates and giveaways.

https://joannewritesbooks.com

About the author.

J.S Ellis is a thriller author. She lives in Malta with her husband and their furbabies, Eloise and Theo. When she's not writing or reading, she's either cooking, eating cheese and chocolate, or listening to good music and enjoying a glass of wine or two.

Website https://joannewritesbooks.com

Facebook https://www.facebook.com/authorJ.SEllis/

Instagram @ author_j.sellis

Goodreads http://bit.ly/2P8a9xx

Pinterest: https://bit.ly/3iqBvrU

Amazon: https://amzn.to/30rbKSq

Bingebooks: https://bingebooks.com/author/j-s-ellis

Bookbub: https://www.bookbub.com/authors/j-s-ellis

Secrets and Lies J.S. Ellis

Made in the USA
Las Vegas, NV
14 February 2023